Tony Dickenson is an English teacher working in international education. He attended Georgia State University in Atlanta, graduating with degrees in English Literature and Applied Linguistics. His interests include teaching, learning, the study of Latin languages and discovering new parts of London, the city in which he lives.

A la curiosidad – lo que me das, me hace volar

Tony Dickenson

PUFFIN BOY

AUSTIN MACAULEY PUBLISHERS™

LONDON • CAMBRIDGE • NEW YORK • SHARJAH

A CIP catalogue record for this title is available from the British Library.

ISBN 9781528905497 (Paperback)
ISBN 9781528905503 (Kindle e-book)
ISBN 978152895 8004 (ePub e-book)

www.austinmacauley.com

First Published (2019)
Austin Macauley Publishers Ltd
25 Canada Square
Canary Wharf
London
E14 5LQ

Dr A Segura

As you set out for Ithaka
hope your road is a long one,
full of adventure, full of discovery.
Laistrygonians, Cyclops,
angry Poseidon—don't be afraid of them:
you'll never find things like that on your way
as long as you keep your thoughts raised high,
as long as a rare excitement
stirs your spirit and your body.

We know that we come from the winds, and that we shall return to them; that all life is perhaps a knot, a tangle, a blemish in the eternal smoothness. But why should this make us unhappy? Let us rather love one another, and work and rejoice. I don't believe in this world-sorrow.

E M Forster

1

It's been many years since I left the island off the west coast of Scotland on which I was born in 1942. A remote strip of land, small, just a mile across and four miles long, no matter where you were, you could hear the rush and hush of the mighty Atlantic Ocean sweeping across the island, the taste of its salty breeze always on your lips.

Though it warmed us in summers, as children, island elders told us simple fables that our miserable winters, short dark days of savage storms that battered us relentlessly, often lasting months, were sent by God as punishment for the dishonourable deeds of long-forgotten, ancient ancestors who had strayed from the righteous path of island ways.

Punishing us for the transgressions of dead people made little sense to me as an infant. It still doesn't. And neither did distressing stories of a Europe, so close by, destroying itself.

But not even World War was able to disrupt the rhythm of life on our impoverished little island. If it weren't for the occasional tiny planes, the Luftwaffe, high in the sky, either heading to or returning from bombing raids in Glasgow, Edinburgh, or the shipbuilding town of Clydebank, places as foreign to me then as Berlin or Paris, I doubt we would have believed the stories of the sickening barbarity unfolding on the continent.

Simply put, the island wasn't worth bombing. We had nothing of any value. We were poor before the war, during the war and certainly so in the years following that unimaginable upheaval.

Original islanders, proud and gentle Picts, always had the sea to protect them from outsiders. So, it must have come as quite a shock to those on the beach that day in the sixth century when a boatload of gentle Irish monks sailed in to tell them strange tales of a strange God who offered not only eternal salvation for all, but the possibility of another life in paradise after they toppled from this mortal coil.

These holy men, a busy lot, quickly built an abbey to praise their god. In it, they kept beautiful gilded books in which they wrote of their unshakeable devotion to him and this fleeting, earthly experience. These historical artefacts established the island as a centre of Christian learning which, over the centuries, has attracted medieval scholars keen to learn of life in a shadowy, ancient past.

After a few scuffles with the indigenous population a couple of hundred years later, the Vikings took over in the eighth century. They, too, quickly made themselves at home, dazzling primitive islanders with their skills in boat building, earthenware, leatherwork and smelting, relics of which are still regularly uncovered on the island today.

However, not all visitors were seduced by the natural beauty of our island. In 1773, hoping to explore this great centre of Christian learning, Samuel Johnson, creator of the English dictionary, arrived. On seeing the wretched state of the inhabitants, he left immediately, declaring my ancestors 'remarkably gross, remarkably neglected', and that 'only two of which could speak English and that not one can write and read'. Thankfully, over the next couple of hundred years, we smartened ourselves up, and though Gaelic was still widely spoken, English finally, just about, managed to worm its way in, and since Johnson's brief sojourn, island life has been relatively uneventful.

During the summer months of my childhood, the ferry brought supplies three, sometimes four times per week. It also brought people, just a handful—strangers, mainly religious pilgrims and scholars, outsiders with foreign ways we were warned to avoid.

Father grew particularly anxious as summer approached, making it crystal clear through stern lectures that under no circumstances was I permitted to speak to anyone not of the island. Following his advice required little effort on my part.

Visitors rarely veered off the short walk from the harbour to the abbey, exchanging little more with locals than polite nods.

Occasionally, however, a more adventurous type, normally alone, would wander up onto the cliffs where I spent a good deal of childhood sketching, and compliment me on my drawings, our brief exchange always very pleasant.

It was up on the cliffs where I was happiest, especially in early May when hundreds and thousands of puffins returned to mate, my favourite time of the year.

But despite the natural splendour of the island, there was a darker, more ominous side to this windswept rock on the margins of a crumbling continent. A side that differed greatly from serene, carefree days, sitting among the puffins idling away my time.

As a boy, I lived in two distinct worlds. The first, and most spectacular, the unspoilt beauty of the island, the cliffs, the sea, the puffins. The second, a world in which an invisible, looming threat, constantly lurking, sucked from islanders any glimmer of joy, leaving them in a permanent state of misery, always cautious, always anxious, always unhappy.

To escape this gloom, I sought sanctuary on the cliffs, away from a home in which the sun rarely shone, where I was always aware of a constant, unrelenting threat from a sad and lonely man. My father.

I was obedient, did well at school, yet I'm certain he despised me. Always unhappy and lacking any trace of paternal tenderness, he smiled only in church on Sundays. Buried deep within him, a disturbing, dangerous anger simmered, so severe that from infancy, I unconsciously absorbed a strict, unspoken code of how to be when in his presence. Silent. Obedient. Invisible.

And, as far back as I remember, I knew *I* was the reason for his unhappiness. Now a father myself, I shudder when I think back to the way he sometimes stared at me, a haunting glare so threatening, it terrified me, making me feel very much an intruder. Unwanted.

But Mother wanted me. I always knew life for her with him was desperately hard. I always wondered why she married him. He barely talked to her, and when he did, it was to snap frustrations of his dissatisfaction with me, and so, she suffered him with nervous impatience, her hands always trembling in his presence.

On one occasion while up on the cliffs, I lost all track of time, and late for dinner, ran home as fast as I could. My late arrival resulted in a beating so severe, his belt buckle exposed the bone in my ankle, rendering me unable to walk for days.

A year or so later, as I helped Mother wash dishes, a glass slipped from my hand and shattered across the kitchen floor. In a fit of fury, he leapt from his chair, picked me up by the neck and roared his disgust at me.

Though she rarely intervened, Mother did so this time, screaming for him to release me, screams I still hear today, pulling desperately at his arms, pleading with him to stop. I still bear the scars where the sharp and searing shards pierced through the skin of my back when he threw me to the floor and continued to thrash me. Though Mother tried her utmost to restrain him, he was too strong, so she fell to her knees and shielded me with her body.

For a moment, I heard only his breathless wheezing before suddenly, he let loose again, Mother screaming hysterically as he flogged her, each strike of his belt across her back making her body jolt, then flinch rigid, his mauling abruptly ending not out of mercy, but from exhaustion, and he stormed from the house.

Brief respite came for us both when he was at sea, often away for up to a week, delightful days only tainted by the thought that, inevitably, he would soon return. I'm not sure if other boys on the island endured such cruelty, but, like me, they too were expected to follow their fathers to sea and become fishermen. As our providers, our main source of food, we were taught to revere these men, and through rousing stories of mythical sea battles which we heard frequently at school, we learned of the heroic, yet often tragic sacrifices made by generations of fine island men lost at sea. Those unfortunates who never made it home were never forgotten, always with us, watching us, immortalised in black and white photographs hanging on our classroom walls, reminding us of their ultimate sacrifice. Reminding us of who was expected to replace them.

The few words my parents spoke to each other were in Gaelic, a language my father spoke exclusively. But in his absence, from the few books Mother had inherited from her aunt, she read me enchanting bedtime stories in English, wonderful, forbidden sounds, beautiful English words, whispered to me as I drifted off to sleep, somehow making the magical, exciting lives of children having incredible adventures in make-believe worlds even more fascinating. When Father returned, she read these stories with one eye on the door, slipping the book under my pillow if she heard him moving in another room.

She couldn't have known what lay in store for me during my teenage years, but those stories, telling me of happy people leading happy lives, not only told me of life beyond the island, but instilled in me a love for language which proved instrumental in preparing me for events during a turbulent adolescence.

And her books feature in another fond memory from my childhood. I was five or six, and seeking diversion one dreadful winter's day, I carried the books quietly from the shelf in the sitting room to my bedroom. Though I could barely read, I had great fun thumbing through pages, trying to decode the mysterious black shapes, convincing myself that the most exciting story I was *reading* aloud to myself, was really being generated by the page I was staring at.

When I grew tired of this, I stacked one book on top of another until I'd built a tower as tall as me. Then, stomping up and down in front of it, I quivered with excitement as my literary tower swayed and trembled, each stomp threatening to bring it down. But it proved sturdy, refusing to crumble, so I cheated, nudging it with my belly, and as the books came crashing down around me, I leapt onto my bed and bounced away in sheer delight.

Many years later, on my first trip back to the island from university, alone in the house, I thought back to that day. Mother's book collection had grown considerably since my childhood, bookshelves bending under the weight of books which included countless volumes of poetry, a collection of Shakespeare plays, a few Greek and Roman tragedies and many works by Jane Austen and the Bronte sisters.

When I suddenly saw again the book with the mauve cover lined with a gold border, the one that had taken pride of place on top of my tower that day, I pulled it from the shelf and read its title, embossed in gold on its cover, a moment of not only warm nostalgia but one of utter disbelief.

When I first read *Lady Chatterley's Lover,* those passages so sexually graphic in nature made my skin prickle, and I understood why the government saw fit to ban it.

A few years later, in the early 1960s, this book of such impressive notoriety was creating a stir both at home and abroad, central to an explosive legal case in London challenging archaic free speech laws which fortunately, the publisher won. But how, I wondered as I held the book, had a copy found its way into our home.

I flicked through the pages reading the small notes Mother had scribbled in the margins. When she returned unexpectedly, I slipped it back onto the shelf and though intrigued, I thought it probably best not to ask her how this copy had ended up on a bookshelf in our sitting room.

By the time I was twelve, the year my most marvellous adventure began, stories Mother had read to me as a boy, of wonder and adventure beyond the island, had begun to fade. As with most boys at that age, simmering inside me were thoughts of my future. However, as a boy, as an islander, I had few choices. Like boys of previous generations, like my father and his father before him, my course appeared set. My destiny was the sea.

But fortunately, that destiny was interrupted.

However, before I tell you how that came about, I must first tell you of what I saw from the cliffs one afternoon a few months before that terrible beauty, the Atlantic Ocean, battered the island yet again with the most magnificent storm, one that steered my life in an altogether most wonderful and different direction.

2

My earliest memory is of a warm summer's day, the sky full of a beautiful blue. I'm three, maybe four, with Mother on the cliffs, near to where the puffins nest, and overhead, gulls swoop and clack as if part of our game. Mother is chasing me, my little legs never quite fast enough to escape her sudden clutches that scoop me up, and I scream in wild delight as she whispers that now she has me she'll never let me go.

At six I am sent to school. This sudden, monumental change in life, an undeserved punishment, a shock so severe, it signalled an end to tender days of childhood joy. I was extremely unhappy.

A crumbling old building made of island stone, the school had only two classrooms. One for infants, one for juniors, and a draughty assembly hall that also functioned as a dining room.

The headmaster never smiled. Like a sinister character in a Dickens' novel, he passed his days loitering, watching, like a phantom slipping into classes unannounced to startle many of the younger students who, looking up from their books to see him among them, burst into tears.

In those days, the concept of school as a place to nurture young minds, to fulfil unlimited potential, would have puzzled the elders running the island. They considered the school's primary purpose to mould us into adult islanders capable of enduring the grim journey that lay before us. And to achieve this end, school guided, instructed, infused in us, a disciplined resilience we'd be calling on regularly for the rest of our lives.

But nurturing such resilience wasn't solely the responsibility of the school. Much of what we learnt there was also fervently repeated in church, and at home, a tripartite effort to embed in us stringent codes of conduct necessary for communal island living, the teacher, the minister, our parents, pointing us in the same direction, preparing us for a subdued life of conformity, of drudgery, of mystifying silence.

On Sundays, in church, the minister warned us what to avoid and what to fear. He assured us that the devil was always near, ever vigilant, always watching, moving in mysterious ways as he taunted us, tempted us, tricked us into revealing our natural wickedness.

He repeated these threats on Mondays when he visited school, terrifying us with disturbing stories of island children long dead. He appeared to enjoy telling us of their suicides, drownings, sudden mysterious disappearances, graphic descriptions of terrible tragedies that befell those island boys and girls too weak to resist temptation, the devil coming, stealing them, then tossing them into hell.

And he revealed how God had created our island in the image of heaven itself. Those wanting to abandon it, leave its magical shores for the wicked ways of the mainland, were already on that slippery slope into the devil's clutches, and unless they quickly changed their ways, they, too, would suffer the torment of eternal damnation.

And until I was twelve, I believed every word he said.

While the church warned of supernatural dangers, at home, I was warned of real-life dangers living among us on the island. When Father first told me of the *spectre*, a madman who lived on his own in the southern part of the island, I innocently asked why he lived alone. A dark fury suddenly quivered up through him and he slapped my face, thundering a simple warning that if *ever* I mentioned that man again, or stepped within a mile of where he lived, he'd kill me himself.

A few days after issuing this threat, it seemed he was intent on keeping his promise. I arrived home from school and he was waiting for me just inside the door, his belt dangling in his hand. I turned to run, but he was quick, catching me by the collar, dragging me back inside and roaring that I'd been seen wandering in that part of the island near to where the spectre lived. It wasn't true, I pleaded my innocence, begging him not to beat me, that he was mistaken. But a queer and bitter hatred had taken hold of him, my innocent cries drowned by his own angry lament that I, his only ungrateful son, was little more than a wretched liar.

He raised his fist but Mother stepped in, grabbing his wrist with both hands. He momentarily glared at her, thundered a howl of such exhausted frustration, then punched her face, the force of his strike making her legs buckle, and, as if in slow motion, she collapsed, her head striking the kitchen table on descent, her body slumping to the floor with an ominous thump.

Certain he'd killed her, I scurried across the floor to her. She groaned, stretched out her trembling arms and pulled me in, the two of us screaming for mercy, remaining wrapped around each other until he stormed from the house.

On a sunny June day, a year or so after that terrible event, I really did see the *spectre*. I was up on the cliffs sketching puffins as they flapped between the sea and their nests, small hollows in the cliff face.

Looking up from my sketchpad, I saw a movement on the shoreline in the distance, a horse, bolting through the breakwater. On its back, the striking figure of a shirtless man rocking precariously, his milk-white torso hunched over the horse's mane as if whispering in its ear. At such speed and riding bareback, I waited for him to tumble, but he possessed remarkable self-control, a graceful self-assurance, and when he slowed to a stop, the horse, knee-deep in waves on the beach below me, lying flat on my chest, I peeked out over the cliff edge.

I'd never seen him before so knew immediately it was the *spectre*. I always imagined that seeing him would be a terrifying moment. But it was quite the opposite—a moment

I've never forgotten, this almost celestial vision instantly mesmerising me.

Crowned with a mop of thick red curls, his athletic physique suggested he was in his mid-thirties. Leaning forward, he patted the horse's steaming neck, his back glistening in the midday sun. As if in a moment of mediation, he sat staring out at the ocean before the horse waded slowly, deeper into the waves. Scooping up water, he splashed it on the horse's neck, and ran his hand over its coat, smoothing it out. Then, turning, the horse plodded south, back along the beach, the way it had come, the sun on the man's back glowing like a beacon. He stopped at the small path leading to the inner part of the island. Like a Gallic warrior, he turned the horse around, and sat motionless looking back down the beach as if searching for something. When he raised his hand, as if in salute, I thought perhaps he was shielding his eyes from the sun. But then, I'm sure he looked up towards the cliff edge, to where I lay hidden, and tentatively, he raised his arm, holding it aloft, as if waving.

3

There was a lonely boy in my class who never talked. We all knew why. Mother assured me his father had not abandoned his family. He'd simply gone to the mainland in search of work. She added I was to ignore ugly rumours that the boy's father had gone mad, rowed out into an Atlantic squall one dreadful winter night and was never seen again. And I was to be kind to him.

Islanders who left the island rarely returned. Those who did come back, mainly old women, did so either to die in the place they were born, or, like Mother's aunt, return out of family obligation, in this case to look after her.

Like my father, the boy's father was a fisherman. He didn't need to leave the island to find work. So, the morning I got up and Mother told me that Father had left for the mainland, I assumed he'd be gone forever.

During his absence, it was always a pleasure to arrive home from school to hear Mother cheerfully humming to herself. Seeing her so relaxed, happy even, I had to constantly dispel a shameful hidden desire that made me warm with delight when it came to mind; that my father would be gone forever. And so, when I arrived home from school one afternoon a few days later to see him sitting in front of the fire, my heart sank.

He shifted uncomfortably in his chair when I entered. Glaring at me, he said nothing. Mother nodded for me to welcome him home which I did. *Normal* family life had resumed.

On the kitchen table was a brown package. Smiling feebly, Mother told me that Father had brought me a present from the mainland. Again, she nodded for me to thank him. He responded with a muffled grunt.

Sitting at the kitchen table, Mother and I examined the package.

"Go on, open it," she said, pushing it towards me.

I tugged at the stubborn knot which slid quickly into a snarled and tangled ball. She fetched scissors and snipped the string, her eyes lighting up when the wrapping fell loose and a grey woollen arm of a jacket slumped across the table. She flattened out the remainder of the packaging to find inside, along with the jacket, a matching pair of trousers. She snatched the jacket out, rushed around the table, and yanking me from the chair, held it across my chest, then spinning me round, wrestled me into it.

"You'll be the smartest boy in church on Sunday," she said, dropping to her knees to roll up then pin the hems of the sleeves.

But there was something else hidden within the crinkled packaging. Reaching in, I pulled out a dark blue and green hat with a small woollen ball, a 'toorie', hanging loosely in the middle of its crown making it look much like a tea cosy. I recognised it immediately as a tam o' shanter, the type of hat seen frequently in Scottish pastoral paintings from the eighteenth century. When Mother saw it, she sprang up, puffed it out and planted it on my head. When it slipped down over my eyes, she stifled her laugh, rolled up its edges, tilted it a little, then placed it back on my head.

Trying to unravel a stubborn knot in a thin rope, Father looked up, nodded weakly, and muttered a warning that I was to take good care of that hat.

The following morning, almost out of sight of home on my way to school, I heard Mother calling me from the door to return. She disappeared inside, reappearing moments later holding the hat. I stepped back shaking my head, protesting that only 'old men' wore such hats.

We both saw the sudden shadowy movement behind the curtain, Father watching. Reluctantly, I lowered my head. She rolled up the edges of the hat and put it on me, but moments later, shortly after rounding the curve in the lane, I took it off and stuffed it deep into my bag.

Neither school nor our home is there now. Even so, when I return to the island, even in the dreariest weather, I always stroll the three miles that took me to school each day. When I see again those narrow lanes of ancient stone walls laboriously stacked by generations of islanders, I feel once more that gentle sense of solitude I knew so well as a boy.

Back then I thought I was growing up in the loneliest place on earth. But years later, while wandering deserted country lanes in Galicia, in northwest Spain, I experienced a similar sense of solitude in that ancient verdant landscape, dissected with similar stone walls like those that shaped my island, and I felt very much at home.

I spent a glorious month with a family who told me charming Galician folk tales that reminded me much of my own childhood experience on the island. Aside from the language, the only significant difference in their stories were descriptions of sun-scorched Galician summers, endless blue skies, wispy warm days, dusty lanes, quite unlike the temperamental, unpredictable whims of Scottish weather that we islanders always bore with a shrug. When I shared with them stories of my island, particularly the story of that ferocious and unexpected storm that rushed in off the Atlantic one day to change the course of my life, as I told it, as it always did when I recounted events of that day, it sounded hard to believe.

On that day, like most days, a stiff wind was whipping up off the sea across the island, whistling through the cracks in the roof of the school building. Late afternoon, during the final lesson, torrential rain and howling winds made the building suddenly darken and groan. The schoolmaster did his best to continue the lesson, but when a heavy object, possibly the branch of tree, suddenly struck the roof and plaster rained down on us, we scrambled below our desks and remained there shivering, many of the girls crying.

Tapping his lower lip with his index finger, the schoolmaster crossed the room to the window. Looking briefly up at the dark clouds swirling in a low mischievous sky, he ordered us out from below our desks and dismissed us half an hour early.

He knew Father well—they spoke often at church on Sundays—so I made sure he saw me wearing my hat as I left. Moments later, as I sprinted through the playground, it flew off my head, high into the air, a whirling wind carrying it, keeping it aloft. When I finally caught it, I glanced back to see the schoolmaster watching me through the classroom window. I placed the hat back on my head, and so it wouldn't fly off again, held it down with one hand and with my bag in the other, raced off down the lane.

From behind me, growing in strength, the wind drove me on. Once or twice, I nearly lost all balance and stumbled. When conditions unexpectedly worsened, the rain suddenly turning into a torrent of hail, small freezing pebbles pinging up off the tarmac, the lane a sudden blanket of white, I ran on, head down, and though frigid air scorched my lungs and small frozen pellets nipped the back of my neck, on and on and on I ran, doing my best not to lose my balance. Or my precious hat.

But then came an almighty blast from behind, so forceful it momentarily lifted me into the air then sent me sprawling across the icy sheet, my schoolbag flying out of my hand and landing in the ditch running along the foot of the wall.

But, luckily, firmly within my grip, my hat.

I struggled to my feet and ran on, the deafening howl of the wind screaming in my ears, until, strangely, suddenly, it died and I slowed to a stop.

Looking up at the dark, rolling clouds still moving swiftly across the sky, a gentle breeze, like one blowing up off the sea on a warm summer's day, swept over me.

I wrung the hat out, then turned back to fetch my bag, but a sudden invisible swell, one of such ferocity, tackling me from the side, again lifted me into the air, much higher this time, before releasing me, and I came crashing down, heavily, on my chest, about a yard from the wall.

I have only a vague recollection of lifting my face up out of cold mud. I rolled slowly onto my back and opened my eyes. Rain blurred my vision but I could still make out the dark swollen clouds rushing across the sky. But there was something else too, hovering about thirty feet above me, a small dark spot, a trembling orb, one moment dropping, the next, shooting up like a kite jerking on an invisible string. I thought it perhaps a bird's nest dislodged from a tree, but when it dropped to about ten feet directly above me, somehow suspended there spinning in a current of air, a sudden terrible panic crashed through me.

That small dark spot was my hat.

I'm not sure how long I lay there watching it. But I had to get it; I couldn't go home without it.

When it dropped onto the wall, snagging itself on a sharp flint, I struggled to my feet and staggered towards the wall. Reaching for the hat, just as I almost had it, a sudden gust unhooked it, and it flew off into the field behind.

I hoisted myself onto the wall to see it quivering in the wind. I jumped down, stooped to pick it up, but again, it suddenly flew up, high into the air, dropping in the middle of the field, tumbling across the sodden grass, and much to my annoyance, sailed over another wall at the far end of the field.

Trudging through the mud, I heaved myself up onto the wall, startled by the sudden appearance of a horse's long face. Dark, kind eyes blinked at me as it released a soft snort. Sleek, muscular, indeed quite magnificent, much like a racehorse, I slowly reached out and stroked its mane.

When I slipped down into its enclosure, the horse suddenly shot off, bucking, jumping, cavorting like an excited foal, tearing around the field until finally, it stopped by my hat. Looking up at me, it nudged the hat with its nose, and again, caught in another gust, it shot up into the air, landing at the far end of the field next to a gate behind which there was a small cottage.

Cold, wet and exhausted, I slogged across the muddy field, stopping about ten feet from the hat. Then, as if trying to corner a small elusive animal, I stepped softly, slowly towards it, praying it wouldn't fly off again.

And when the wind dropped, I rushed in.

4

I wake in a small room. There are books. Hundreds, maybe thousands of books. A library? It's hot; I hear the crackle of a fire. My head throbs. On my forehead, a bandage. Light, from a small window, shines in. The walls are books. On a small table, papers, in piles. And more books. A small statue, a slender ballerina, her long graceful arm extended. On the floor, a gramophone. Above it, hanging on the wall, next to a small door, an accordion. A draught whistles down through the chimney. Orange flames turn blue. Wind shakes the window.

A noise. From behind the door. A floorboard creaks. Someone's there. At the door. It inches open, a sudden scratching, a scurry, a sprint, a leap, a small dog, on me, panting, licking my face, its tail, a little motor, frantically wagging.

"Mot. Mottie. Leave the boy alone. Get down," says a man dipping in through the doorway carrying a tray, steam swirling from the spout of a porcelain teapot.

I know him. The horseman. It's the spectre.

He rests the tray on the chair next to the small table.

"Mottie! Down!" he orders.

The dog jumps to the floor and sits at my feet. Whining, it stares up at me.

"I'm sorry about Mot. We have few guests here. When we do, well, as you can see, he tends to get a wee bit overexcited," says the spectre, stooping down to snatch the dog up and cradle it in his arms.

The dog licks his face and he laughs loudly.

"Are you OK, son? You're not hurt, are ye? Mottie found you out cold, by the wall. You must have stumbled into it," he says, pointing to the bandage on my forehead, the dog rushing back to me when he puts it down.

He wears an apron smeared with glistening paint, oil paint. And a small cap, tweed, its peak worn and soiled. His shirtsleeves rolled to his elbows reveal the tan skin of his arms. His eyes remind me of the horse. Gentle. Playful. He hums as he pours tea.

"I'm fine. Thank you," I say.

"I dressed it up as best I could," he says, pointing to my forehead and handing me a cup of tea. "It'll do until you get home."

He pats his leg. The dog scampers across the floor, leaps into his lap and stretches out. The man strokes the groove below its long jaw.

"I'm Thomas. Don't get many visitors down this part of the island. Fortunately, my reputation takes care of that," he says, a smile rising in his handsome face.

"I'm Tom. I think I lost my hat."

Wind shakes the door. Rain speckles the window. We sit in silence.

He puts the dog down beside him and stretches towards the gramophone. He flicks a switch. A momentary crackle before a deep bass sound fills the room. Bagpipes, their haunting drone, magical, mystical. He plants the dog in his lap, leans back in his chair, closes his eyes. The dog, its chin on its paws, watches me. I close my eyes and sink into the sounds of the pipes.

When the music stops, I open my eyes and see the man's arm reaching towards me. In his hand, my hat.

"I cleaned it up as best I could," he says. "Not seen a tam o' shanter in many a year."

I look around the room. Books everywhere.

"I brought them back with me from university. Edinburgh. Beautiful city," he says, standing and pulling a book from a shelf. "Tom, son, somewhere in one of these books, a clever man wrote how to live a good and decent life. I'm still trying to find it," he continues, laughing to himself. "This side of the room is literature. Shakespeare,

28

Burns, too many to mention," he says pointing to a shelf on one side of the room. "On that side, science," he says nodding at the other. "Come through and I'll show you the rest," he says, disappearing through the doorway, the dog rushing after him.

I follow him into a large spacious studio, into a kaleidoscope of colour, light spilling in through two large skylights in a high wood-beamed vaulted ceiling onto hundreds of paintings, all of the island, hanging on every wall. Magnificent paintings of places I know. Different parts of the island.

He's an artist.

On opposite sides of the studio, more shelves sagging under the weight of more books.

"Music, composers, singers on this side," he says, pointing to shelves on one side of the studio, "art and great artists on those," he adds, pointing to books on shelves on the other side, their tattered spines smudged with paint.

In the middle of the studio, there's an easel. On it, a canvas. The paint is wet, glistening in the light. I immediately recognise the stretch of beach below the cliffs. Where I sit with the puffins. Where I first saw him riding his horse.

"Tom. Why are we here?" he asks.

"You asked me to come through," I say, thinking his question odd.

"No, son, why is man here?"

I don't know what he means.

"How old are you, son?"

"Twelve."

"Tom, do you know what a philosopher is?"

I shake my head.

He leads me to the far end of the studio and pulls a dusty cover from a canvas. It's a painting of my school.

"This is where I went to school. You must go there too?" he says.

I nod.

"What do you learn at school, Tom?"

I think for a moment.

"We read the Bible. The times tables. And Gaelic," I say.

The sparkle in his eyes fade.

He crosses the studio to a cupboard covered by a sheet. Whipping it off, he momentarily disappears in a sparkling cloud of dust, reappearing holding a small easel. He opens it out and places it in the middle of the studio next to his. He returns to the cupboard, rummages inside and pulls out a small blank canvas.

"Tom. What do you see on this?" he asks, smiling.

"Nothing. It's blank," I reply, again puzzled by the question.

"And what does a blank canvas need, son?"

"Colour."

"Exactly," he says, still smiling. "And so, it's time to begin," he continues, handing me a small metal box full of pencils, crayons, paintbrushes. "Draw me something," he says, nodding toward the canvas.

"I can't draw."

"Have you ever tried? Don't they teach you to draw in school?"

I shake my head.

He tuts, mumbles something about school and trots back to the cupboard. He returns holding a small white apron, and as if presenting me with a prestigious medal, he places it over my head and fastens it behind me.

"This was mine, when I was a wee boy. Aye, I was about your size at your age," he says, placing his hands on my shoulders and turning me towards the easel.

I look at the canvas. My mind, much like the canvas before me, blank.

"I don't know what to draw," I confess.

"Don't worry, son," he says. "Starting is always the hardest part. Once you get going, you'll be fine. Let's see. OK. Close your eyes. Now, just relax. Are ye relaxed?"

I nod, take a deep breath and close my eyes.

"Now, think about this place, this beautiful island. Think of beauty, Tom, think of your favourite place on the island.

Where you're most happy, where you feel most alive. Where you feel most like yourself. Are you there, boy? Can you see it?"

"Yes," I reply excitedly, and suddenly, I'm up on the cliffs, among the puffins, looking out at the big blue Atlantic stretching across the horizon.

"OK. Good. What do you see? What's around you? How do you feel? What's in front of you? Do you see it, son? Tell me what you see."

"Puffins," I say, "puffins," I repeat, breathlessly, opening my eyes to see Thomas smiling, holding a magazine, on its cover a photo of a puffin.

"Here," he says, "this'll help you get started, Puffin Boy!"

He leaves the studio and returns moments later followed by the beautiful voice of a soprano.

"Mary Gardner," he says, "the most famous Scottish singer of all time."

He heard her sing in Paris. And side by side, he paints and I draw. On a blanket between our easels, Mot sleeps. Occasionally, Thomas helps me. Gentle suggestions. Sometimes, he guides my hand with his.

Late afternoon. The storm has run its course. Sunlight streaming in through the skylights fades. We inspect each other's work. His painting is colourful, precise. He's an artist. Though still a simple outline, he nods approval of my puffin.

"You'll have to come back and finish this," he says, stepping towards the canvas. "You have real potential, son."

"I will," I say instinctively, though I know a return visit impossible. "I'd better get home. Mother will be worried. I won't tell her I was here," I say, suddenly wishing I hadn't.

At the door of the cottage, Thomas shakes my hand and thanks me for coming.

"Oh, wait one moment," he says, slipping back inside, returning with my hat. "Don't forget this."

Mot walks at my side to the field gate. The horse snorts and shakes its mane.

"What's his name?" I ask, stroking its head.

"Tom," Thomas says smiling.

The horse follows me to the wall at the far end of the field. I turn to wave goodbye but Thomas has gone.

5

A heavy rain was falling as I approached the house. I'd tell them I sheltered from the storm in the crumbling lighthouse on the cliffs, where Mother sometimes took me as an infant. It sounded reasonable.

I fixed the hat on my head and opened the door. Mother, her eyes red and swollen, rushed towards me, wrapping me in trembling arms.

She wiped the hair from my eyes, and in hers, I saw that worried, anxious look I knew so well. She turned and looked at the dark apparition lurking by the kitchen door. Water dripping from his clothes, a small puddle at his feet. Dangling from his clenched fist, a belt.

I rushed out my feeble excuse as Father stomped towards us, Mother turning towards him, her hands gripping my arms, pushing me back towards the front door as she screamed at him.

"You will *not* touch my child," she cried, her back taut, trembling, her fingers tightening around my forearms as she edged me further into the corner of the room.

"Get out of my way, woman," he roared at her, their noses almost touching.

"You shall not touch my child," she roared back, refusing to budge, her stiff body unwilling to give him access to mine.

She screamed when he raised his fist, her body shaking as he thundered a string of Gaelic curses. Then, in a fit of desperate rage, he turned and brought his fist crashing down onto the kitchen table, kicked over a chair, and stormed out of the house, raging at himself as he slammed the door behind him.

Exhausted, Mother collapsed into a chair at the kitchen table. Burying her face in her hands, she wept.

"Run along to your room," she whispered moments later, drying her eyes, getting to her feet and looking out the window.

Worried he'd take out his frustration with me on Mother, I sat in my room with the door cracked open, waiting for him to return.

I thought back to that afternoon, to meeting Thomas. Of what he'd said about the beauty of our island. And about being happy. Such a kind and thoughtful man.

Father returned. Sat in his chair, he stoked the fire. Mother asked him if he wanted dinner. He grunted a response.

Thomas. A gentle, interesting man. Why was he called the *spectre,* I wondered? Such a callous, undeserving reputation. And was he not lonely living such a solitary existence? He seemed happy. He laughed. He had Mot, he painted, he explored the island. Perhaps his isolation was self-imposed? Perhaps, somewhere in one of his books, within those thousands, millions of pages, he'd already found instructions on how to be happy?

And as these thoughts rushed through me, I suddenly realised that amid the grey, unhappy lives that most islanders led, one amongst us shone. He had rainbows in his life. I saw them in his eyes, I heard them in his laugh, I felt them in the way he held Mot and in the way he spoke to me.

But what *was* it that made islanders so cautious, guarded, so frightened? Why *was* there no joy in their lives?

Entrenched in his own furious little world, I thought again of the turbulent temper, the fury constantly simmering in my father. Had he ever been happy? Why did he hate me? Why did he beat me? And how could he treat Mother as he did? This rampant anger, this rage, constantly rattling him. From where did it stem? And how, day-in, day-out, could he bear such a burden?

And Mother? Had she *once* seen him smile? Had a moment of tenderness ever slipped from him? Had they ever laughed together? Was it me who had driven them apart and brought despair into their lives?

But this malaise, this general state of gloomy melancholy rested in all islanders. The minister, so unsmiling, the teacher, always so harsh.

And then, as images of my father, the minister, the teacher, raced through my mind, the most deeply disturbing thought suddenly overwhelmed me. In fact, it was a moment of sheer terror when, for the first time, I realised that I was part of this flock, I, too, was buried deep within this ancient island weave, an invisible, insignificant thread in a joyless fabric, plodding blindly, sadly, along a well-worn plank generations of islanders had trodden for centuries. And my descent had already begun, I could feel myself slowly slipping, sliding, sinking, into a desolate and desperate void. From which there was little chance of escape.

I thought of how islanders simply surrendered, allowed happiness to passively slip from their lives. But not Thomas. He knew what happiness felt like. He'd escaped. Taken a different route. Somehow, he'd found a way out. Unlocked something in himself that, perhaps, I, too, might possess. That perhaps, I, too, might unlock in myself.

In that chance encounter, he'd unearthed something in me, something that no other islander had come close to stirring. I had to see him again. I wanted to know what he knew. I wanted to paint with him, read his books, listen to his music. I wanted to feel Mot's tongue licking my face. I wanted to know how to lead a good and decent life. I wanted to be happy.

I thought again of the puffin I'd started to draw. Much of the canvas still remained blank. It required colour. Orange for its beak and little webbed feet. A shiny black for its little fledgling wings.

6

The year I met Thomas, the month of April was delightfully warm. The temperate but unpredictable Gulf Stream that brings the west coast of Scotland its inclement weather slipped south into England, dumping on that country the rain we usually received. With days growing longer, I ran to the cliffs after school each day and sat on the cliff edge searching the skies over the ocean, waiting for that magical moment when the first puffins return from wherever they go in winter months.

That year, however, I found myself looking southward, down towards the shore, to where I'd seen Thomas galloping along the beach.

I imagined seeing him again. He'd stop on the beach below, wave up to me, then take the small path up from the beach and invite me back to his cottage. I'd thank him for taking care of me on the day of the storm, for tending to my forehead, for showing such kindness, and we'd spend the remainder of the afternoon painting. I'd add colour to my puffin, I'd give it life, a rich orange for its beak and feet, a shiny black for its little body.

The pleasant weather continued into May. By the middle of the month, the puffins had returned, thousands of them swooping in and out to sea, the cliff face alive with chatter. Though delighted to be back among them, a strange impatience continued to trouble me and I found myself constantly looking searchingly south, along the shore, hoping to see a horse racing down the beach.

Towards the middle of the month, a simmering desire to see Thomas again had grown into one of restless frustration, a feeling I knew would linger and groan within me if I didn't do something about it. So, I made a bold and daring decision: I would return to see him.

On the third Saturday of May every year, islanders assembled to discuss the sober nature of island management in the small hall next to the abbey, about an hour's walk from home. My parents attended this event each year; they'd be gone all day, and so, I chose that day to go and see Thomas.

On the morning of the meeting, idly flicking through the pages of a book at the kitchen table, I monitored my parents' movements as they got ready. Only on this day, though begrudgingly, and only for this gathering, did Father tolerate Mother wearing makeup.

When she announced they were leaving, I looked up and barely recognised the beautiful young woman standing over me, her eyes sparkling a warm blue, cherry-red lips, redder than I'd ever seen. She kissed my cheek and reminded me to eat lunch. Standing at the door in a grey suit he wore only to church and funerals, Father told her to hurry up.

I waited fifteen minutes before I left for Thomas', taking the same route through the fields as I had on the day of the storm. When I jumped into the last field, again I was met by the horse, who ran to me, snorting, shaking its mane.

About fifty feet from the cottage, I saw the door crack open and Mot, whining with excitement, come scampering out, squeeze under the field gate, and yelping feverishly, dashed towards me, jumping up into my arms and licking my face.

"Tom, my boy. What an honour and pleasure to see you again," said Thomas, standing in the doorway, oil paint on his apron glinting in the morning sun, a broad grin making his cheeks colour. "And Mottie's missed you too," he said, releasing a deep booming laughter. "Come on in, son, and thank you for bringing the most beautiful day with you. I'll make tea."

Moments later, he returned from the kitchen with a tray piled high with cakes and a pot of steaming tea.

"I was a little concerned after you left and the wind picked up," he said, brushing the hair from my forehead to examine the fading scar. "Well on the mend," he added as he poured the tea.

"I came to, well, to thank you for helping me during the storm," I stuttered.

"Oh, son, no thanks required. It was a pleasure. Like I told you, I rarely get visitors so, I was glad of the company. You're welcome anytime," he said, handing me a cup.

"I thought, perhaps, that I could finish my puffin, the painting I started," I said sheepishly.

"I'm glad to hear it, son," he replied, a smile rising in his eyes.

"Who taught you to paint, Thomas?" I asked.

He didn't respond immediately. Collecting his thoughts, he drew in a deep breath and patted his thigh for Mot to jump into his lap.

"Tom, I've always felt a profound connection with this island; it's where I belong. I left for a while. To go to university. In Edinburgh. Fine city. But I soon realised I longed to be home. Even today, on the odd occasion, I visit the mainland, I'm itching to return. When I was a boy, about your age, like you, I used to roam this land with my father. My love for my father was, well, like my love for this island. He instilled in me a deep appreciation for the natural magnificence that surrounds us. He taught me first to draw, then later, how to paint. He insisted I use the beauty of what's all around us, here on this island, as a source of inspiration. My mother had died when I was just a bairn, and when he died, I was fifteen; my mother's sister, my aunt, a delightful woman, quite unlike other island folk, came back from the mainland and took me in, and I came to live here. This was her home. The studio wasn't here then, I built that myself after she died. I remember the look of surprise on her face when I arrived with a cart load of paintings, all of them of the island, quite a number of puffins too, like the one you've started."

"Where are they now? Can I see them?"

"Only if you go to Edinburgh," he said, grinning at the puzzled look on my face. "And you'll need permission. You see, my aunt saw in me, well, in my paintings, a talent I certainly didn't see in myself. I'd been out of school a couple of years; I really didn't know what to do with my life. Without telling me, she sent some of my paintings to a friend of hers, secretary to the dean at the university in Edinburgh. He saw potential in them, in me, and invited me to Edinburgh, to discuss taking up a place. As far as I know, no one had left the island to study at university before. Normally, those who left, had to, to find work, and they never came back. The day the letter from the university arrived offering me a place, my aunt danced around the house. Word soon spread about my good fortune. And of my imminent departure."

He drew in another long, deep breath.

"My aunt, such a decent woman, was so proud of me. As we did every week, we attended Sunday service the following weekend. I doubt church has changed much since then, the minister's warnings—the dangers of sin, temptation and other such nonsense. On that morning, however, his sermon was longer, with even greater emphasis on the wicked ways of the mainland. Sound familiar?" he said, looking up at me.

I nodded.

"Well, that day in his sermon, he informed the congregation exactly *who* was responsible for the immoral ways of the world, and *where* the worst sin flourished. The sin and the sinners, he pronounced, were on the mainland, in institutions of higher education. Universities in Glasgow and Edinburgh. Boys, he declared, should be taught to be men, to work the land, fish the seas, follow and appreciate the traditions of islanders who, through the generations, have sacrificed much, many their lives. And in these troubled times today, he said, where wicked greed and desire constantly linger, those who *willingly* avoid our ways, our work, who *choose* to leave the island for the mainland, for cities, for these institutes, to pursue more *delicate* and *vain* vocations, were on a slippery slope to eternal damnation.

"To be honest, I wasn't quite sure what he was getting at. I'd been listening to such drivel all my life and tended to drift off during his sermons. So, I didn't see it as a personal attack. But my aunt, God rest her soul, she saw it for what it was. And she was having none of it.

"When I felt her hand take mine, and she stood up and pulled me into the aisle, I didn't know what she was doing. Neither did the rest of the congregation, everyone staring at us. The minister stopped talking, and my aunt, glaring at him, cleared her throat, and in language more fitting of mainland infidels, she informed him that the only one on this island going to hell was him, and we stomped out. I've not stepped foot in the place since.

"Like I said, I was too young to understand. You don't expect a minister, a stalwart of the community to use his position, his *power*, to publicly shame and humiliate us, me, like that. But I understood the gravity of my aunt's transgression. I knew that by her challenging the perceived wisdom of the church, of challenging the minister, this font of righteous virtue, meant that from that day on, we were 'dead' to other islanders. She said she didn't care what others thought, constantly assuring me that neither should I. The poor thing, well, I don't know how she managed on her own, especially after I left for Edinburgh.

"As September approached, nearly time to leave, I should have been looking forward to a new and exciting life on the mainland. But I wasn't. I wasn't sure if I'd leave. If I could leave. The island was all I'd ever known, it felt part of me. It was where I belonged.

"But my aunt knew me well. She saw in me a slow reluctance; a remoteness I couldn't disguise. She wasn't about to let me waste such an opportunity. So, she went to Edinburgh, spent a fortune on course books, came back, dumped them in my lap and suggested I get started."

"Why didn't you want go?" I asked.

Leaning forward, he inspected his palms and drew in another deep breath.

"It's true, I didn't want to go," he said. "I didn't want to leave the island; I knew nothing else."

He rested his elbows on his knees and, again, paused to gather his thoughts.

"But there was another reason why it was hard to leave. A reason my aunt knew nothing of. I told you that everyone on the island ignored us. That's not quite true. There was someone who didn't. A girl. One day, when I was up on the cliffs, near to where you watch the puffins, she came up to me and said hello. I recognised her from church. A couple of years younger than me, still at school, she'd been in church the day we'd stormed out. But she said hello. The only one."

He looked up at me.

"You don't know *that* girl. I've no idea what became of her," he said, wringing his hands, a tremble in his sigh. "We began to meet, in secret. Not even my aunt knew. Well, I fell in love with her and wanted to stay. For her. I loved her so desperately. But what future was there for us here? We couldn't go on as we were, meeting in secret, not on this island. As summer drew to a close, I thought of my aunt, what she'd sacrificed, all for me. I couldn't disappoint her, and so I had to go, gutlessly convincing myself I was leaving for the girl's sake. If people found out she was seeing me, she'd live a lifetime of shame. For someone so young, so innocent, she could never bear the humiliation my aunt experienced. No one deserved that."

He drained the tea from his cup.

"Of course, it was a coward's way out. Not a day has gone by that I haven't thought of those last words that passed between us. The tears, the heartbreak, watching her walk away, rejected. God, I felt so ashamed. Still do. I'll always carry that burden with me. When I left the island, I vowed never to return, a sort of penance for what I did to her.

"After graduating, I stayed in Edinburgh for a few years, teaching art in a school, but then my aunt died and left me this cottage. When I came back, I felt again that deeply rooted connection with the island, so I stayed.

"But islanders have memories like elephants. They never forget. And they never forgot what my aunt said to the minister that day in church. And so, I inherited her life of isolation, and bear a reputation a good, good woman, never deserved. I'm alone but happy, that's what's important. And, the truth be known, I'm glad they leave me be. These books, my painting, music, these keep me company now. I go to the mainland once or twice a year, mainly Edinburgh, sometimes Glasgow, to pick up paints, books, music…"

Mot suddenly barked.

"Oh, but Tom, my boy," Thomas said, apologetically, "don't think for a moment you're intruding here, son. Believe me, if only you knew what it means to have you here, to talk to you, to get to know you. Anyway, enough of this dreary business. Come, come with me, I want to show you something," he said, leading me into his studio, Mot scampering behind us.

He'd made small changes to my drawing. Minor adjustments, improvements, extending the wings, just slightly, narrowing the bill, and widening the webbing on my puffin's feet. On a small desk beside my easel, he'd arranged a number of small paint pots.

"Tom, I think your puffin needs colour. Getting the colour, the shading just right, getting it to blend in on canvas, and in life, can prove difficult; it takes time," he said, pausing. "But, as you did before, use your imagination. Trust it, go with what you feel is right. If you need help, son, just ask me," he said, and then nodded towards my canvas.

For the next hour or so, as Thomas brought life to the stretch of beach below the cliffs, I brought life to my puffin. "Do you know this part of the beach, Tom?" he asked.

"It's where I watch the puffins," I replied, "my favourite part of the island."

"Aye, mine too. It's where I met that lass I told you about. Where we said goodbye, too. Strange, how such beauty can summon such sadness…" he said, snapping himself from further reflection, announcing it was time for tea.

Back in the sitting room, surrounded by books, we drank tea as Mot, sitting obediently between us licked up any stray crumbs that fell to the floor from our chunky cheese sandwiches.

"Tom, do you remember the question I asked you on your first visit?" Thomas asked.

I remembered him mentioning something but I couldn't recall the question, and shook my head.

"What is a philosopher? Do you remember?"

I nodded. "Do you know what it means?"

I shook my head.

"It's about thinking. Thinking about how one should live."

"Like fishing?" I replied.

"Well, yes, and no. Think about it like this. You're just a wee boy now, but think about, say, ten years from now. Imagine yourself looking back then. Imagine what your life will be like. How do you think you'll feel about what you've achieved? Will you be happy?"

I'm not sure I understood what he meant. I'd never given any thought to being an adult. Like most islanders, I assumed my future fixed, and like Father, I'd be a fisherman; I'd go to sea.

"Do you think you'll ever leave the island, son?"

"I'd like to visit the mainland one day. Mother's aunt lived in Edinburgh for many years, but she came back to take care of her."

"Aye, son, in praise of kind old aunts! The island has a way of pulling you back. Who knows what the future holds, for any of us. But, son, if adventure presents itself, take it, it's a big world out there."

"Father says I'll never leave the island. He says the mainland's full of thieves and drunks. The minister says cities like Edinburgh and Glasgow is the devil's work."

"Your father and the minister must be brothers," said Thomas laughing.

Mot scurried across the room and jumped up into his lap.

"Son, sometimes I think the devil's here on the island. Have you ever noticed how unhappy people are?" he said, the tone of his voice shifting.

It was true. Most islanders were a dreary bunch, satisfied with simple routine, leading a beleaguered existence.

"Have you heard of Plato, Tom?" he continued.

A name from a comic book I'd read? Not sure, I shook my head.

And with that question, our journey began. A journey on which Thomas would guide me, gently, purposefully, provide me with a singular education that would bring beauty and unimaginable treasures to a young mind ready to venture, to reconsider, to re-evaluate everything I'd ever been told.

"Well, let me tell you a little about him, about what philosophers do. Along with Aristotle and Socrates, more about those two later, Plato was a Greek philosopher who lived thousands of years ago. Imagine that, Tom, with all our modern ways, we're still learning how to live decent lives from men who lived thousands of years ago. Plato talked about how we, people like you and me, can *choose* to live our lives. He talked about how people *find* happiness. Listen, you're just a wee thing now, but we have to start somewhere. So, let's just chat. And don't forget to ask questions. I'll be asking you plenty! So, now, let's see. OK, let me ask you. Is it better to be happy or sad?"

"Happy," I responded, thinking my response obvious.

"Well if that's *really* the case, then why do so many islanders *choose* to be sad?"

I thought of Father, of other islanders, drifting through life in a rarely-changing state of smouldering misery. I think I understood what he was getting at. That perhaps people were, somehow, deliberately unhappy?

His question awoke something in me, something I'd been thinking about since the day I met him. A question that over the years I've continued to ask myself, one that to this day continues to challenge me to think about life, and how to live it.

Thomas proved to be the most exceptional of teachers. He introduced new concepts with such zeal, as if he himself were discovering them for the first time. We discussed ideas of great men and women who, throughout the millennia, had challenged conventional thinking. Artists, pioneers, visionaries, breaching new frontiers, proposing and promoting new ideas to seek new ways of thinking, new ways of seeing, new ways of living. They celebrated the wonders of their own and others' human ingenuity, helping us to evolve, to get along, helping for the greater good of us all.

I remember when Thomas first mentioned Darwin. The possibility of man evolving from a lower species, primitive beings, both shocked and captivated me. Through the years, either loosely or directly, we frequently returned to discussion on the origins of man. Like most people, I'd always assumed God, in his mysterious ways, had masterminded us being here, so this alternative version of events was a lot to absorb. To his credit, Thomas *did* mention the possibility of the divine having something to do with getting the universe up and running, though somewhat half-heartedly.

He said that Homo habilis, or 'nearly' humans as he described them, was the first stage of what would evolve into Homo sapiens, modern man. We looked at illustrations in the encyclopaedia of the different stages of humans evolving, the earliest on all fours, the ape, tree dwellers. The most important shift, certainly for us, when they came down out of the trees to explore the short grasses of the savannah. Ever fearful of being eaten themselves, their survival required constant vigilance, so up they went, on two legs, wandering the plains in search of food, always on the lookout for hungry, prowling carnivores. And simply put, they remained upright. They never came down.

Thomas read aloud the likely time periods at which each stage of evolution had occurred, not only in humans but in other species too, these changes sometimes taking millions of years.

In the months that followed, I read more about Darwin, about the possibility of us once being apes, and the more I explored, the more I could see how such changes, quite possibly, might just be true.

But understanding new concepts, new ways of thinking, was hard work. It required considerable effort on my part. Gradually, I began reflecting on the many other *truths* I'd acquired in my brief life, constantly asking myself questions about everything I'd ever learnt, about what I'd been told; and as I did, little by little, day after day, I found myself unravelling, reassessing everything that, up until that point, I'd considered to be true.

Truth was important. It required evidence. In both his personal life, and within the scientific community, Darwin, a well-respected Victorian, had suffered ridicule for his ideas, for a *truth* in which he believed. He questioned the role God had played in creation and, like Thomas' aunt, for standing up to the pulpit bully, had been cast out. By seeking the truth, great men like Darwin (and women like Thomas' aunt), understood that if conventional thinking was at odds with the truth, then it needed to be challenged. It needed to be changed.

Another seismic shift came when Thomas told me that for most of human history man had lived without the wheel. Again, sensing my doubt, he rummaged in his desk drawer and produced a lump of chalk. Then, slumping to his knees, he drew a long straight line across the floor, a timeline on which he subdivided important events that had occurred on our planet over time, marking on it undisputable, remarkable moments in human history where, as humans, we took great leaps forward. The wheel, he said, was one such leap, an extraordinary discovery occurring somewhere in the Middle East, probably by a potter who, intuitively, thought his wheel might be put to a better, greater use than making simple pots.

As Mot ran up and down the timeline sniffing at the chalk dust, I studied the different points in time, geological and historical moments of such magnitude—dinosaurs, meteors, Homo habilis, at *people* in between, Neanderthals, their demise, our rise. To be alive for most of human history sounded very dangerous, very bleak. So much death, destruction, decay. So much suffering. I felt lucky to be born in the twentieth century.

I visited Thomas once, sometimes twice a week throughout my teenage years. As I made my way to his cottage, I was always so excited knowing that on my way home later that day, I'd be thinking about something new, often thinking about it for days, until the next visit, when we'd talk about it, and, as always, he'd leave me spellbound by just how much he knew about everything.

In later years, our discussions shifted to difficult, intangible concepts about the human condition. When we talked about love, hate, jealousy, of which I had little practical experience, he constantly reminded me to stop him when I didn't understand. I *had* to ask questions. A concept, a word, any aspect of discussion that hindered my understanding, that required clarification, I *had* to seek clarity, I *had* to ask. And when I appeared lost, which was frequent, his comforting words assuring me that, 'son, no one's born with the knowledge', always made me feel less awkward.

He was a super teacher; he knew exactly what he was doing. Yet, at times, our discussions, especially those concerning nebulous, abstract concepts, rarely resulted in a satisfactory conclusion. This frustrated me. As did his constant probing of my responses with more questions, a technique that required of me to give more profound consideration to these concepts which, no doubt his intention, eventually, helped me grasp thorny, difficult ideas, ones which at first seemed impossible to crack.

As with the timeline, he often used simple analogies, pictures, perhaps a piece of music, or, as he'd done with evolution, draw visible representations, diagrams, charts, in fact any and all methods that would provide a new way of considering the topic in question. Other times, he left me alone to search in his books for answers myself. When I made an exciting discovery and read it aloud to him, he clapped with joy, praising me with such fervour it made my skin tingle.

Sometimes, as I read, every so often, he'd stop me mid-sentence and ask me to read back to him, a single sentence, or part of a passage. Then we'd pick it apart, unravel it line by line, eke out its deeper meaning. Slowly, a recurring thread that connected many of our discussions emerged, one that linked back to the question he'd asked me on that first day, about the pursuit of a 'good and decent life', about how we find happiness.

A technique I found particularly frustrating involved him introducing an exciting new idea at the end of the day, just as I was leaving, packing me off home to 'think about it for next time'. He used it the first time, and to great effect, on that day I returned to see him.

It was getting late—I wanted to be back before my parents returned from the meeting, and just as we were finishing our tea, again he mentioned Plato and the allegory of the cave.

"What would you do in a cave without light?" he asked.

"I'd try to get out," I replied.

"But what if you'd been in the cave so long, it was all you knew? No one inside the cave had ever stepped outside, just generations of people living in the dark, believing that only danger lay outside. Would you go out into the light? On your own?"

When he put it like that, I wasn't so sure. He then suggested that within our lifetime man would probably build a rocket and go to the moon. I considered this unlikely.

"Would you go up in it?" he asked.

"No, I wouldn't. It wouldn't be safe."

"Who then will be the first to go up? Someone has to be the first. Think about it. Fifty years ago, for most people, the idea of flight was inconceivable, that man building a machine that took to the air was absurd, impossible," he said, getting up and pulling a book from the bookshelf.

He thumbed it open to a page with pictures of two dapper gentlemen in smart suits, more like stockbrokers than inventors, Orville and Wilbur Wright, leaning against what looked more like a crate than a plane.

"Rudimentary, I know," he said, looking at the picture with a sense of awe. "But they gave it a go. Took a risk. Yes," he said, looking momentarily through the window, "someone always has to be first."

Mot suddenly barked.

"Well, that's enough for today," he said. "You'd better be on your way, it's getting late. You can finish the painting next time you come, OK?" he said, looking at me.

I smiled, nodding my appreciation.

On the way home, I thought about the Wright brothers, truly brilliant men. A little mad perhaps, but certainly brilliant.

That night, I lay in bed trying to imagine uninterrupted darkness deep inside a cave. I fell asleep and had the most marvellous dream. I was strapped into a fantastical rocket blasting off to the moon, and then, miraculously, I was floating in a big silver can in space. Below me, through one window, the beautiful blue earth, and through the other, twinkling into forever, millions of stars.

But the dream came to an abrupt end around dawn when I woke with a start, my heart pounding. I dressed quickly, snuck out, sprinted up the lane and through the fields to Thomas' cottage and thumped the door. He appeared in his pyjamas holding a steaming mug of tea.

"What is it, son, everything OK?" he asked as Mot dashed out, whining, trying to climb my legs.

"Thomas, Thomas. I understand," I said excitedly. "This is my life. This is my story. To be happy, I have to leave the cave. Thomas, I got it, I got it, I got it. The island's the cave. I'm going to leave the island, I'm going to the moon, I'm going to see the stars," I said, turning and running back through the field.

"Well, don't be leaving anytime soon," he called after me, "we've only just begun."

7

My enduring memory of that first summer, when I went to see Thomas every day, is Shakespeare. And his most famous Scottish play, Macbeth.

The first of many of the bard's plays we read over the years, we had fun acting out key scenes, interpreting them in any manner that pleased. I particularly enjoyed playing the furious Macduff at the end of the play, chasing Mot, an unwitting Macbeth, around the room in the hope of lopping off his head. Thomas' portrayal of Lady Macbeth was so convincing, in both verbal and physical perniciousness, it made me think of my own sense of lofty, vaulting ambition, and the risk I was taking by leading such a secretive double existence.

These were golden years in my life. I wanted to know about everything. What created wind? Why the sky was blue? Why I felt cold?

On some days, we went outside and looked up in wonder at the sky, at clouds, at birds, insects. Other days, we looked down, into the soil, digging deep into the dirt to see what we might find. We examined the rock on which I'd so fortunately stumbled on the day I chased my hat, and Thomas explained that the flint tip jutting up out of the earth, much like the tip of an iceberg, was simply the peak of an enormous rock buried deep within the earth below.

My curious mind so alert, so alive with wonder, I carried a small notebook in which I wrote down questions constantly springing to mind and then discussed them with Thomas.

Yet, still, hanging over me, always, the fear that my parents would unwittingly learn of my deceptive double life.

If this were to happen, then I'd never see Thomas again, crushing my ambitions for a happy future. My life would be over.

And so, especially in that first year, to make sure I remained undetected, I took great care not to be seen on my way to his cottage, frequently stopping, turning and doubling back to check I wasn't being followed. Other times, I'd sit on the beach, often for more than hour, before taking the small path up past his cottage, and even then, I wouldn't enter immediately, but walk on, half a mile or so, and return only when I knew it was safe.

Strangely, what I thought might arouse suspicion was my school report. Most years, I normally finished third or fourth overall, a satisfactory ranking for parents who rarely asked about school. However, the first report I received after I began meeting Thomas had me ranked top of the class. But such improvement only brought on new worry, I feared that so sudden a change, an academic leap so meticulously detailed in a glowing report, might alert them, especially Father, to activities in my life outside of home. This in turn would raise suspicion, give him reason for greater surveillance, and so I made sure that nothing appeared different in my life. I arrived home, more or less, at the same time each day, and remained the quiet, obedient son I was expected to be.

And I remember vividly the day I received that first outstanding report, the day we broke up for summer, students trembling in their seats as the headmaster passed slowly up and down the aisles handing out terrifying brown envelopes containing details of our achievements that year.

I handed mine to Father later that day and waited patiently as he read it. When his face grew dark and he sighed disapprovingly, I wondered what comment he'd read to evoke such a negative reaction. Mother, monitoring proceedings from the kitchen, flinched when he thrust his arm into the air and waved the report at her.

Sitting at the kitchen table, she inspected it quietly. When she finished, she drew in a deep breath, folded it, slipped it back inside the envelope and put it in the drawer alongside previous reports.

"Tom, I'd like to see you outside," she said, a serious look of disappointment on her face.

I followed her outside where she threw her arms around me and kissed my forehead over and over again, tears of happiness welling in her eyes.

"Oh, Tom, my boy. You're top of the class. You're the brightest boy on the island," she said, kissing my forehead again and swinging me around. "Now, go on, run along and play. Go and watch the puffins. I might join you later if I have time," she said and disappeared inside.

The following year, as was customary, again Father read the report first. Again, he sighed and shook his head in derisory fashion before waving it dismissively at Mother. And, like the year before, she calmly read it then asked me to step outside where she hugged and kissed me for once more coming top of the class. She asked me to wait a moment, she had something for me, and disappeared inside.

As I waited, I thought of my father's adverse reaction to my glowing report. How could such exemplary performance warrant such cold response?

And then, suddenly, quite unexpectedly, I realised why.

Had the report detailed my attempts to set fire to the school, or that I was regularly torturing infants, he would have been none the wiser. He didn't understand a word, the mystifying shapes in the report meant nothing to him.

My father was illiterate.

Mother returned holding a small packet wrapped in brown paper tied neatly with a white cotton bow. Nervously, I opened it to find inside a small copy of Shakespeare's Macbeth.

"It's Shakespeare. A Scottish play," she said, surely unaware that it was my favourite Shakespeare play, of how much that particular play meant to me after having so much fun performing it with Thomas.

So moved by her kindness, doing my best not to cry, I thanked her over and over, and later that afternoon, sitting among the puffins, I read it again, and to this day, that copy of that play remains a most prized possession.

Discovering my father's illiteracy changed my feelings about him. He had spent a lifetime surreptitiously guarding a private shame, one so cumbersome, one he endured alone, I had no doubt this burden had in no small way shaped him into the troubled and bitter man he became. From then on, I felt a curious blend of both sympathy and pity for him, and I saw him for what he was, a sad man spinning in a lonely, solitary world from which there was no possibility of escape.

One afternoon, that summer, I found Thomas in his studio, a large map of Great Britain rolled out across the floor. Pointing to a speck of land just off the northwest coast, our little island, he said that millions of years ago it had been part of the mainland, but through shifting undercurrents deep in the earth's core, it had broken off. In fact, he added, that all land on the planet was once connected, just one solitary landmass, a supercontinent, Pangea, and that the turbulent energy, constantly rumbling, rifting in the planet's core, cracked open that single landmass to form individual continents. In a similar way, our little island, once connected to the mainland, had broken away.

I wasn't convinced.

He assured me this was the case, that Scottish geologists had compared rocks on our island with those on the mainland to show them identical. He fetched another map, of the whole world, and rolling it open over the other, asked me to look at the continents, to consider the *possibility* that these enormous landmasses, at one time, were connected. He fell to his knees and running his hand along the east coast of South America, asked me to study its shape. Then, skipping across the map, he ran his hand down the west coast of Africa, again asking me to regard its shape and compare them, for me to imagine the world as a jigsaw, to think for a moment if these two enormous continents, roughly, at one point, might have been part of a whole.

I remained unconvinced, so he folded the map, making the South Atlantic Ocean disappear so that Africa and South

America appeared, more or less, side by side. And only then, in a moment of geological wonderment, did I concede that indeed these landmasses, thousands of miles apart, just *might* have once been joined.

So impressed by this new, fascinating discovery, and now convinced that the world, albeit slowly, was shifting below my feet, I looked for my own evidence on the beach the following day.

The first pebble I found, small, beautiful, polished a smooth cool green, had me thinking of its journey from the centre of the earth, through the millions of years, and into my hands—this little gem the first and most prized in a collection which grew rapidly.

I maintained this occupation throughout my teenage years, and spent the morning of my fifteenth birthday scouring the beach below the cliffs for other such beauties. With lunchtime approaching, I headed home, plodding back up the cliff path planning to return after lunch.

At the top of the path, I stopped to catch my breath. I could just about see smoke trickling from our chimney, and oddly, gathered outside, a small knot of people. With Father away at sea, I thought Mother had had an accident, and somewhat alarmed, I hurried home.

When the small throng, mainly women, saw me, they released a terrifying wail, swarming around me and ushering me inside, into the sitting room, where more women sobbed loudly.

Sitting in Father's chair, Mother's weary pale face was smudged with tears. At her sides, as if guarding her, fishermen shifted uncomfortably when they saw me. Her handkerchief twisted into knots, she wiped her eyes, looked up at me and got to her feet. Drawing in a deep breath, she led me to my room and told me that Father was dead.

She provided few details, saying simply that there had been an accident at sea.

However, at school a couple of weeks later, about to enter the classroom, inside, two boys whose fathers had been on the boat, were discussing the events of that night.

Lingering outside, I listened, and found out exactly what had happened to my father.

The catch that day had been huge. At around midnight, as they did most nights, the men gathered below deck for a communal meal. Besides the bountiful catch, they had good reason to celebrate that night. The day before the men left for sea, one of the younger fishermen had become a father to a healthy son. Though frowned upon on land, the men drank at sea, whiskey, and that night, everyone was in high spirits. Except Father.

He remained quiet, distant, saying nothing. Though some of the men tried to lift his mood, he left the gathering early, bidding them a whispered goodnight, and they gave no further thought to whatever was troubling him.

An hour or so later, one of the boy's father alerted the others of an emergency on deck.

The men scampered up to see my father shivering in the frigid sea blasts, a ghostly pale figure at the front of the boat, naked, looking at them with a wild, haunting stare, mumbling to himself.

They pleaded with him to step back, to think of his wife, his son, but he didn't seem to hear, and when one of the men rushed towards him, he stepped back, the choppy dark swells instantly swallowing him, and though they searched through the night, at first light, the fishermen returned to the island.

Two days later, the island community gathered in church for a service of remembrance. As the minister tried to lighten the mood with brief childhood anecdotes of happier moments in my father's life, alone on the front pew, Mother and I held each other's hand.

After the service, Mother maintained a serene sense of dignity, standing with the minister at the church door, shaking people's hands, thanking them for coming. When the last had gone, while she spoke with the minister, I loitered outside and saw in the distance the silhouette of a man on a horse. About to raise my arm and wave, Mother called to me, it was time to go, and together, we walked slowly home.

In the days following the service, she remained withdrawn, her mood hard to gauge. We spoke little, ate meals in silence, and during afternoons and evenings, she sewed, knitted, or attended to menial household duties.

Neighbours, mainly women, occasionally stopped by with small gifts. One kind elderly woman brought a black shawl, the type often worn by women after the loss of their husbands. Mother thanked her and broke down in tears, the only time I saw her cry.

The following morning, I awoke to see her sitting on my bed.

"Tom, let's go to the beach and collect rocks together. We can look at the puffins too," she said. "Like we did when you were small. It will take our minds off of things."

After breakfast, I fetched my bag from my room, returning to the kitchen moments later to see her wearing her best coat, the one she normally wore to church. And even more surprisingly, she was wearing makeup.

We took the narrow path down to the beach, walking half a mile or so before the wind picked up, rain began to fall, and so we made our way home.

When I reached the top of the cliff path, I glanced back to see Mother had stopped, about halfway down, looking back along the beach, as if searching for something.

8

Mother had never talked to me about her life as a child. I knew nothing of her parents, or the brief life she had before she married. However, on long walks together, often to parts of the island I'd never seen before, from time to time, she'd let slip a detail about an event in her childhood, or perhaps a character she admired from a book she'd read. She spoke frequently about her aunt who'd returned from Edinburgh to raise her when her parents died, and stopping one morning outside a small cottage, long-abandoned, crumbling, no roof, the front door missing and stones on one side of the building plundered, she told me it was where she was born. We didn't stay long.

One aspect of our new life together I particularly enjoyed were long afternoons spent reading, perfectly content in each other's company. Occasionally, I'd look up from my book and see how rested she looked. Sometimes, a smile appeared in her eyes sending a warm swell of emotion rippling through me. I liked being with her. At home, at the beach, on long walks. I liked seeing her no longer have to worry about sudden volatile outbursts from a strange husband.

But these balmy days of warm intimacy ended one afternoon when she announced I was returning to school, the best moment of my first day back, a most dull and uneventful day, the sound of the bell releasing me to run and see Thomas.

His welcome, more subdued than usual, he shook my hand and invited me in. As he made tea, Mot sat patiently by the fire, his sad little eyes watching me. When I called him, he darted across the room, sprang up onto my chest and licked my face.

Thomas brought in the tea. He stoked the fire, passed me a cup and slumped into his chair.

I wanted to talk to him about a matter that I'd been wrestling with ever since Father's death.

On so many afternoons, inspired by a new discovery or at last having understood what initially appeared an impossible concept, way beyond my understanding, I often walked home from his cottage tears welling in my eyes. Neighbours had flocked to our house wailing for a man they barely knew. But still, I had yet to shed a tear for a dead father. And what worried me most, I didn't think I would.

I felt guilty. I thought there was something lacking in me. Empathy, compassion, an inability to succumb to emotion, a fundamental aspect of our humanity which Thomas and I had spoken about so often. And yet, I couldn't grieve. I simply felt nothing. And I needed to know why.

I'd read many of John Donne's poems with Thomas, and had been thinking about one in particular, Sonnet X, about death. I recalled its opening lines.

Death be not proud, though some have called you
Mighty and dreadful, for, thou art not so

Thomas had said that death connects all humans, rich or poor. Worrying about it is pointless, that we need to 'push on' that such 'interruption' is temporary, fleeting, especially in the young. If we permit such a natural event in life's cycle to linger within us, to consume us, we diminish the quality of living a good life, of living in the here and now. As humans, he added, we constantly question and doubt ourselves. We judge ourselves too harshly, especially when confronted with difficult moments in life. Like the death of someone close to us. Such moments, though tragic, are simply part of the human experience. The best, the *only* thing to do, is depend on each other. Talk to each other.

"Are you OK, son? I'd say it was a bit of a shock?" Thomas asked.

"I saw you from the church," I replied.

"How are you? How's your mother holding up?" he said gently, sincerely.

He'd never mentioned Mother before.

"I've been out walking with her. We've been up on the cliffs. She used to take me there when I was a baby. She said being there reminded her of beautiful times."

"Are *you* OK though, son?"

"It's strange. I should feel terrible about losing Father. But I don't. I haven't cried. I still don't feel like crying. I don't think I will," I said, drawing in a deep breath. "Am I terrible for feeling like this, Thomas?"

Quietly, he waited. He sensed I had more to say.

"Thomas, I don't think he liked me. He never talked to me. He was cruel. He hit me. He hit Mother. Why did she marry him?" I continued, feelings I'd had all my childhood suddenly spilling out into words, my confession startling him.

"No, no, son. Of course not, you're not to think like that. Not at all. I'm sure your father loved you very much," he said, leaning forward in his chair. "You know the ways of island folk, especially men. There's something in us, in me, in you, our little secrets we keep to ourselves, secrets we never share, never speak of. Not even with those closest to us. Your father, God rest his soul, well, only he knew his secret. That's just how some men are. For good, for bad, just the way we are."

"Have you secrets, Thomas?" I asked.

He leaned back in his chair. Mot lay asleep in his lap.

"I certainly have regrets, son," he answered.

Placing Mot on a cushion in front of the fire, he poured more tea.

"Tom. There's no script to follow here, son. There's no rulebook to tell you how to feel, how to act, what to think. Grief can be heavy, and for many people, well, they say nothing, they keep it all in. Tom, I don't have the answers for this. I don't think any of us do. But above all, you must know that you're a good boy, your mother is proud of you, of this I'm *quite* sure. Sometimes, it's better just to think about the future because, son, time stops for no one. There's only the future. That's all we have," he said, getting up and pulling a record from its sleeve. "Do you know what a requiem is?" he asked, placing the record in the gramophone and lowering the needle.

I shook my head.

Music suddenly filled the room. Mozart, he said, about to die, had composed this piece.

As I listened, I thought of what he'd said. To 'think about the future, time doesn't stop'.

Talking to Thomas about my father's death certainly helped, and with his words still swirling through me, I decided, on my way home that afternoon, that from then on, whenever dark thoughts of Father flashed through me, and I felt bitter, angry, I would recall these wise words, think of my future, about living, about leaving the island, about what I had to do to make it happen. And gradually, as days and weeks passed, it got easier. I got on with life. I felt happy again.

Mother never spoke of Father's death. Perhaps, like Thomas had advised me, she thought it better not to dwell on the past. Some things, simply, cannot be undone.

But I began to see changes in her. Quite significant changes. And I remember, almost to the day, when these changes began.

I'd been at the beach collecting rocks and arriving home, heard faint voices inside. However, when I entered, Mother was alone, standing by the back door, a little alarmed at my unexpected appearance. Wrapped in brown paper and tied with string, she was holding a package a neighbour had just brought her. She put it on the table and leaned against the sink.

"Who was that?" I asked, sitting down at the table.

"Oh, just a neighbour," she replied, evasively.

"Aren't you going to open it?" I said, looking at the package.

"I think I'll wait until tomorrow," she replied, a worried look rising in her face.

"Why not open it now?" I persisted.

She sat down, drew in a deep breath, tension still visible in her face.

"Tom, I want to wait until tomorrow. It's my birthday," she said, reaching over and taking my hand.

Suddenly, strangely, it occurred to me that I didn't even know how old Mother was. We'd never celebrated birthdays at home. Not even mine. On that day each year, Mother and I had always celebrated in secret, at the cliffs, an aspect of my childhood I thought normal.

I still clearly remember holding her hand as we made our way to the lighthouse, barely able to contain my excitement because I knew that hidden somewhere below her coat, she had a gift for me. Always a book, one I was desperate to see, desperate to hold. Only once we were sitting comfortably and she'd sung me Happy Birthday did her hand, so slowly, so teasingly, search inside her coat before that most thrilling moment, when a small package appeared, and after I ripped off the wrapping, I lay in her lap looking up into the sky as she read to me.

When it was time to go, she sang Happy Birthday all the way home, and as always, just before we arrived, she reminded me to say nothing to Father, either of the present or my birthday.

I sat on my bed thinking of a gift for her. A painting I'd done as a child. A poem. Something memorable. Moments later, searching through my drawers, I found hidden among my socks, the perfect gift.

Thomas had told me that first beautiful stone I found at the beach, the first in my collection, a little larger than a pebble, pale mottled green and polished smooth over time, was a rare marble, unique to our island. For centuries, islanders believed it had religious significance, the font in the Abbey carved from such rock.

The pebble required little polishing, but all the same, I rubbed it with a sock until it gleamed like a precious jewel, wrapped it in tissue paper and sealed it in an old shoebox. I left it by the door intending to get up early the following day, before Mother, so I could sneak down and leave it on the table to surprise her.

But these plans were dashed by the most wonderful dream, the type of dream in which events feel so real, yet sometimes so worrying that you lay awake thinking, wondering, playing it back in your mind, often relieved that it was indeed only a dream.

In my dream that night, there was music, a delightfully crisp melody I recognised. Schuman's 'Happy Farmer'. I'd heard it many times while painting with Thomas; I knew each note by heart.

I began to hum along, and though almost inaudible at first, gradually, I became aware of another, faintly familiar voice, and suddenly realised it was Mother's, making the dream all the more pleasurable, and I felt myself smiling.

But then I realised I was no longer sleeping, but awake, and looking around my room now full of bright sunlight cascading in through the window. And yet, I could still hear the most beautiful, dulcet sounds of the Schumann melody. In a mild state of shock, I sat upright and knew it wasn't a dream, and that for the first time ever, there was music in our home.

I dressed quickly and rushed to the kitchen to find Mother humming along to music coming from a shiny new wireless on the windowsill.

I wished her a happy birthday and kissed her cheek.

"Isn't it wonderful, Tom? A wireless. Isn't it delightful to wake up to music?" she said, a radiant smile lighting up her face.

She looked puzzled when I handed her the shoebox. We sat at the table and after carefully lifting the lid, she burrowed into the tissue paper until she found the small stone and released a gentle gasp. Then, very delicately, between her index finger and thumb, as if a small, fragile bird's egg, she held it up to light, gazing at it as might a jeweller looking at a rare and valuable gem. Then placing it in her palm, she looked up at me, her eyes brimming with tears and pressed it to her cheek.

"Oh, Tom. It's so beautiful. The most beautiful thing anyone has ever given me. I'll keep it always, I'll treasure it. And one day, when you've left the island, when I'm missing you so much, which will be often, always, always, I'll hold it, like I am now, and think of you. Thank you, son, my good and beautiful son, thank you so very much," she said and kissed my forehead.

And from that day on, there was music in our lives. Each morning, wonderful music, much like the music I listened to as Thomas and I painted. Beautiful melodies. Bach, Beethoven, Mozart, filling our home. It made me so happy. But more importantly, it made Mother happy.

Some mornings, however, as I lay in bed listening to those beautiful melodies, in the distant reaches of my mind, a disturbing restlessness, a brooding, tirelessly rattling, troubled me. When it surfaced, as it did often, I instantly thought of Mother, of how happy she now was, and though I always tried to dispel it, I knew that if given the choice of the wireless or my father in our home, as dark cruel days of my infancy shivered through me, I always opted for happiness.

"Tom. Don't tell anyone about the wireless. Let's just you and I enjoy it. No-one else needs to know," Mother said, kissing me as I left for school that morning of her birthday.

Not telling anyone at school required little effort. Each day, I was growing ever more frustrated with my classmates as they talked excitedly of leaving school, of becoming fishermen and simple housewives like their parents. I had little in common with any of them and so, the daily traipse there seemed increasingly pointless. I learnt everything I needed with Thomas, and most days, I returned home from school complaining to Mother of the teacher, who constantly echoed the minister's message about the perils of any hint of ambition. She said, bluntly, I should be respectful.

As far as I know, Mother had scant knowledge of my intentions to leave the island to study on the mainland. This worried me. Sooner or later, I'd have to tell her, and perhaps even tell her of my forbidden trips to see Thomas. But I dreaded the thought of seeing the disappointment in her eyes. It felt like betrayal.

What sustained me in that final year was Thomas, reminding me regularly that I was to remain focused, that the university entrance examination was in sight, that passing it required discipline.

As I was the only human contact he had, as with Mother, I felt guilty that soon I'd be abandoning him too. Who would he talk to in those lonely moments when I'd gone? Would his life be even more solitary?

Our relationship had always focused on learning. I'd never asked him about life on the mainland, the snippets I'd gathered from our discussions indicating he'd enjoyed academic life, as both a teacher and student. I knew nothing of his personal life. Not until one afternoon, when, after a stirring discussion on the varying merits of martyrdom, I asked him why he'd never married.

I think the question surprised him. He drew in a sharp breath.

"Tom. I never married because of a choice I made long ago, after leaving the island. A choice I regret and must live with every day," he said, pausing, patting his thigh for Mot to jump into his lap. "I told you about the girl I left behind when I went to study in Edinburgh. Well, she was the *only* girl I could ever love. I only realised this after I'd left. On my first trip back, it was too late, she'd moved on. I didn't even try to see her. I didn't want to add further complication to a life I'd already destroyed. I think about her every day, what I did to her. Each day is one of atonement."

He took another deep breath.

"Do you know what atonement is, Tom? I don't believe in paying penance, but I suppose, that's what I'm doing right here, right now. Make sure you don't make the same mistake I did, son. Aye, that was a mistake…" he said, his voice trailing off, memories flickering in his eyes.

There was little chance of that happening to me. I knew little about the few girls on the island. But, once, there had been a girl.

Annabel, a few years older than me. I saw her my first day of school and made sure I always sat behind her in class. So I could stare at her. I'd never seen anyone so beautiful. Skin like porcelain, turquoise eyes the colour of the sea in summer, such natural beauty that boys like me could only admire from a distance.

I especially liked the way her hair fell across her back, and sometimes, when her head tilted back a little, I glimpsed the soft skin of her long neck and the curves of small ears that stayed pink on cold days behind which she rolled stray strands of hair. I wanted to declare my love for her, but at six, I didn't have the words. The closest any such declaration came was the day she turned and looked back at me, sending a wonderfully strange shiver whirling through me as our eyes locked. But clumsily, I dropped my pencil, and after retrieving it, I looked back up but she'd turned back round, my fleeting first experience of love abruptly terminated. Any hopes of my one day marrying her were dashed shortly thereafter when Cameron McLeish began walking her home from school.

By early October, in that final year on the island, two, sometimes three times a week after school, I went to see Thomas, always taking the cliff path down to the beach.

On my way there one afternoon, from up on the cliffs, I saw a woman walking along the shore. Even with her collar up and a hat covering her face, I knew it was Mother. Since Father's death, she often walked on the beach, sometimes finding a stone or a shell to add to my collection, and so, it came as no surprise to see her there.

I ran along the clifftop calling to her, but a brisk, blustery wind rushing in off the sea drowned my voice. I rushed back and took the cliff path down to the beach, running all the way down.

But when I reached the bottom, she was gone.

9

I ran along the beach, past the inland path that led up to Thomas' cottage and followed the shoreline to the southern tip of the island only to find the stretch of beach there deserted. Mother could only have taken the path inland. Up past Thomas' cottage.

I turned and rushed back, storming through my mind the possibility that she might, at that moment, be passing the cottage. As islanders are wont to do, if Thomas happened to be outside, she would politely bid him good day. This courteous nicety would then lead to at first, innocent, casual small talk, perhaps about the weather, or some other trivial topic of conversation, but soon particulars would emerge, of a boy they both knew so well, who had callously betrayed them. Mother embarrassed, humiliated, would finally learn of the deceptive double life I'd been leading for years, of wily subterfuge, of a calculating, reprobate son who she'd never trust again.

I rushed up the path thinking, perhaps, someone had seen me in these parts, had seen me enter the spectre's home, had informed Mother. As my sole protector, she felt it her duty to reproach Thomas, and in doing so, would learn of my terrible transgression, her disappointment, my shame, driving a wedge between us, one that would last a lifetime.

As I approached the cottage, I braced myself, expecting to see them at any moment. What would I say? How, in a moment, such an awkward moment, might I justify to Mother such betrayal?

Creeping through an adjoining field, I snuck up to the cottage and crouched below an open window. Inside, I heard the familiar sound of Thomas stoking the fire and the sudden shriek of the kettle whistling.

I thought Mother must have quickened her pace, passed by the cottage, but about to spring up and call for Mot, I heard the polite clink of a spoon on china, and then, gently, Mother cough.

"Sugar?" asked Thomas.

"No, thank you," Mother replied, a slight tremor in her voice.

The most unsettling sinking feeling plummeted through me. My hopes, my dreams, my beautiful future about to crumble.

"I'm sorry for your loss," Thomas said.

"Thank you," Mother replied.

Somewhere in the distance, angry gulls squabbled.

"I thought I'd be angry. I thought I'd be many things, but now, I'm here, I don't know what to feel. I want to be angry, I really do, but what's passed is passed," Mother said. "I've had a difficult life," she continued, "I had to learn quickly, to be resourceful, to cover the cracks. I would have been ruined."

"I know," Thomas replied, softly, sympathetically, gently clearing his throat.

"I have a boy."

"A boy? What's his name?" he asked.

"Tom, he's a good boy. Bright. Curious. Interesting."

"I'm pleased. Is he happy?"

"He is now. We've had our struggles."

"How old is he?"

"You know how old he is, Thomas," Mother snapped sternly, getting to her feet. "Let's not pretend; I've finished pretending. It's time I left. Tom will be home from school soon. I've said what I came to say. Thank you for the tea. Thank you for the, the…" her voice trailing off as she rushed out.

Mot suddenly appeared above me on the windowsill and barked. I scrambled over a wall and hid.

"Mot, come on, boy, come back in," called Thomas, "I don't think Tom will be coming today," he said, closing the window.

Dusk slouched in off the sea as I walked back along the beach trying to extract meaning from the snippets of their conversation. Clearly, I'd missed a good deal of what they'd said to each other. Why had Thomas feigned knowing me? And why had Mother gone to see him in the first place? From what I'd heard, she knew nothing of my visits there. So, why had she gone? Perhaps someone had seen me near the cottage? And why was she angry with Thomas? None of it made sense.

It was almost dark when I got home. Smoke dribbled from the chimney, the kitchen light was on. Hammering through me, question after question about what they'd discussed, what 'exactly' had passed between them.

I lingered outside unsure if I could lie to Mother if she questioned me about Thomas. I thought of running back to ask him why she'd been to see him. But it was nearly dark; she'd be worrying that I wasn't home.

Mother was in the kitchen preparing dinner. Humming along to the wireless, Mozart's The Marriage of Figaro, his most exuberant, unashamedly joyful piece, nothing in her manner suggested she was anything but happy.

"Hello, Tom. Isn't this the most wonderful music? Dinner will be ready soon," she said, smiling.

In my room, fragments of their conversation tumbled through my mind. I thought of the way she'd spoken to Thomas. Tense, frosty, familiar even. Did they know each other? And why had he pretended not to know me? And thumping through me, again and again and again, why had she gone there in the first place? I couldn't join the dots. None of the pieces fit. Nothing seemed possible, plausible. None of it made sense.

During dinner, Mother's playful mood suggested nothing was amiss. She appeared relaxed, carefree even. She asked about school, if I'd been down to the beach, trivial small talk that only frustrated me more. And still, constantly cascading through me, that question: why had she gone there in the first place?

As she cleared the table, she smiled, again humming cheerfully along to another aria on the wireless. But then, abruptly, she put down the plates, switched the wireless off, and sat with me at the table.

"Tom," she began, pausing to inspect a fingernail. "I need to have a talk with you," she said, looking up, directly at me.

And so, the moment had arrived. What unfolded in the next few moments between us would not only determine the path my life would take, but the honesty of my responses to her questions would in many ways define the person I had become.

Or so, I thought.

"Tom, I'd like to take you to the mainland. To Glasgow. For a couple of days. I think it's time you saw a bit more of the world," she said, her broad smile making her eyes glow.

Unsure if I'd heard her correctly, I remained perfectly still. When she repeated it, confirming what I thought she'd said, unable to contain my joy at this unexpected surprise, I sprang up, rounded the table and wrapped my arms around her, thanking her over and over again, the fear, the worry brought on by her meeting with Thomas, in a single moment, purged.

The rest of that evening remains hazy. I vaguely remember listening to the last part of an opera, thinking of Glasgow, about what Thomas had told me of that cosmopolitan city, an alien world of galleries, museums, cafes. And people, millions of people, so many people. Me going to Glasgow, the mainland. It just didn't feel real.

The opera ended. I hugged Mother, thanked her again and went to my room.

Before going to bed, I briefly returned to the kitchen to fetch my book. Unaware of my presence, Mother was hunched over the kitchen table writing a letter, smiling as she wrote. I thought it best not to disturb her.

After school the following day, I let myself into the cottage. His little tail wagging furiously, Mot bolted into the room and leapt up onto my legs, his excited whiny yelps fading only when I picked him up.

"Tom, my boy, lovely to see you. We missed you yesterday, but no matter," Thomas said, wiping paint from his hands.

He put the kettle on, asked about school, but made no mention of meeting Mother.

"Tom, son," he said. "We need to talk," the tone of his voice suddenly more serious.

I thought that the moment he'd mention Mother, but, thankfully, he had other, more pressing matters he wanted to discuss.

"It's time to start preparing you for the university entrance examination. The hard work must begin now," he said.

My path to a beautiful future still on track, I breathed a sigh of relief.

"Thomas, Mother's taking me to Glasgow," I said excitedly. "Tell me what to do, what to see. I can't wait to see a city. What should I see, Thomas, where should we go?"

"We'll talk of this later; we have to get to work," he said, scooping Mot out of my lap, leaning over me and plucking a book from the shelf above me which he dropped into my lap.

The Wealth of Nations by Adam Smith. He'd mentioned Smith before, but in more general terms. He was a Scotsman, an eminent scholar, an economist, a philosopher, held in the highest regard around the world. Challenging in both scholarly content and size, *The Wealth of Nations* is his most significant work, his legacy.

Thomas was raising the bar.

"Like I said, we need to start. So, read the first chapter. You won't get it all done today so you'll need to take it home, do more there. Homework," he said, smiling. "We'll discuss it next time. Be sure to write down any questions you have," he added, then retreated to his studio for the remainder of the afternoon.

To pass the examination, I had to grasp complex concepts set out in works like Smith's. I had to absorb the material, demonstrate my understanding in essays. This was what examiners needed to see. This is what university required.

The heady world of global economics at first proved difficult. In our discussions, Thomas frequently used terminology like 'labour division'—'production output'—'industry'—so I had a vague knowledge of such terms arising in the first chapter. However, what surprised me most, the number of unfamiliar words.

The first I still remember. 'Opulence'. As in the term 'universal opulence'. I checked the dictionary for meaning then read the passage again, trying to understand the word in context. I read on, noting down words I didn't know, looking up their meanings then re-reading the passages. For words that proved particularly problematic, that I couldn't understand either from the dictionary definition or in context, I tried to use them in discussion with Thomas in subsequent meetings. When I used a word correctly, it thrilled me. He corrected me when I was wrong which helped broaden my vocabulary and solidify my understanding of new words, providing me with a clearer, deeper understanding of Smith's ideas. Exactly the language I needed in essays to impress examiners.

In the first chapter, Smith suggests that 'different seasons of the year set different tasks', that best nations 'tend to have the best-cultivated lands', and the 'wealthiest nations usually outperform their neighbours'. I used these as analogies to spur me on, comparing myself to a nation, a poor one, wrestling with difficult circumstances, knowing that only perseverance would provide me with the outcome I desired. To pass the examination, to be offered a place at university, I had to 'outperform the neighbours'.

So, I worked hard, each visit to Thomas' following the same routine—reading for an hour then writing an essay in response to a question he'd prepared the night before.

At last, it really felt like I was on my way out of the cave.

10

Over breakfast, a week or so later, Mother, quite unexpectedly, informed me we'd be leaving for Glasgow the following day. We ate supper early then went to bed, getting up before dawn to board the ferry just as the sun was rising.

Though bitterly cold, we remained on deck at the back of the ferry and watched the island disappear in the mist. Mother went below deck but I moved to the front, excited to experience that first glimpse of the Scottish coastline.

When a hazy spectral landmass appeared, Mother, suddenly at my side, put her arm around my shoulder.

"Mother, look!" I gasped breathlessly.

"Yes, my love. Where new lives begin," she said, pulling me closer.

A quiet euphoria was crashing through me as the ferry docked. Eager to feel underfoot the sacred soil of the Scottish mainland, as if stepping onto the moon, I felt slightly nervous taking that first step onto another, much bigger island.

This event, however, proved more momentary than momentous. Mother, clearly unaware of the importance of such ceremony, tugged me by the sleeve into the bus terminus, pulling me unceremoniously through the crowd, instructing me to wait with our bags while she bought our tickets to Glasgow.

All around me, chaos. Thick diesel fumes spluttering from buses shrouded the terminus in fog, stinging my eyes and making me cough. Hundreds of people, more than I'd ever seen, rushing frantically every which way across oil-stained parking bays and piling onto buses.

The sudden boom of a man's voice from large speakers in the roof startled me as he announced departures. Tickets in hand, Mother returned, again grabbing my sleeve and pulling me in the direction of the Glasgow bus.

We wound our way along narrow lanes, through beautiful sunlit glens glistening with early-morning dew before joining a larger, busier road. As we reached the outskirts of the city, the blue morning sky had clouded over and a gentle rain speckled the window.

Glasgow's central bus station was much larger than the terminus at the port. And certainly much busier. We collected our bags, dropped them off at a small hotel minutes from the station, and in a cafe nearby, Mother told me of our plans for the day. First, a trip to the zoo. Then, after lunch, a visit to an art gallery in the city centre.

I trembled with excitement at the prospect of going to a zoo, of seeing tigers and lions up close. I'd read of these magnificent creatures in stories, beautiful proud beasts from Africa and Arabia. I imagined them slouching moodily along the sides of their cages eying me up, the soft fur on their backs close enough to touch.

I thoroughly enjoyed my first tram ride to the zoo on the outskirts of the city. I expected to see hundreds of people queuing to get in, but there were no queues, and once inside, it wasn't an animal that first caught my attention, but a beautiful little girl.

Perhaps four or five, dressed neatly in a small plaid coat, she had jet-black hair tied up neatly into a small bun. Her alluring coffee-coloured skin looked so warm, so soft against the milk-white skin of a woman whose hand she held. I'd never seen a black person before. Mother told me not to stare.

Unfortunately, seeing that little girl proved the highlight of my visit. Instead of moody magnificent creatures I'd imagined, we were met with a truly shameful sight, cages full of pitiful jaded beasts, thin and lifeless, their dull fur caked in dirt, their dejected leaden eyes staring blankly into nowhere.

The first enclosure was probably the most distressing. On a concrete island surrounded by a shallow pool, two frail, old polar bears sitting next to each other. I'd seen many photos of these beautiful specimens in books, their glistening fur a brilliant white like the snow in which they tumbled. On these wretched creatures however, their fur, matted with a greenish brown slime, did little to disguise their emaciated state.

In another cage, another deeply disturbing image. A solitary elephant, its back leg tethered by a chain to a ring in a concrete floor. Small, pitiful, watery red-rimmed eyes, two tiny black pearls, wept a voiceless plea. I felt ashamed.

In the next cage: a lonely gorilla. When it stretched its gangly hairless arms out towards me, I told mother I wanted to leave, and on the tram back to the city centre, I couldn't dispel the upsetting images of those animals condemned to lives of squalor, and longed to be back up on the cliffs among the puffins.

Stepping from the tram in the city centre, a man with a large black briefcase knocked me to the ground. Mother pulled me to my feet, brushed me down, and dabbing my hands with her handkerchief, mumbled something about the rough ways of city folk.

In the nineteenth century, Glasgow's golden age, the city was considered a vibrant centre of industry, a glowing example of progress. With few bombing raids during the war, much of its Victorian infrastructure had remained intact, and the grandeur of its fine buildings gave the city a lively cosmopolitan feel. But the golden shine of a century before had long faded, and much like the animals in the zoo, the city looked worn out.

Largely responsible for these grand buildings, and for the city's prestigious reputation, Scotland's most famous architect, Alexander Thomson, who designed the National Gallery of Art, the building we were about to visit.

We had lunch in a small cafe next to the gallery. As I ate a sandwich and drank tea, Mother flicked through the pages of a small address book. She ordered another tea and asked the waitress for directions to an address in the city. Returning moments later with the tea, the waitress handed her directions scribbled on a scrap of paper. Mother slid the mug of tea across the table to me then fumbled in her bag for her makeup case.

"Tom. I have to go somewhere. I won't be long. You're old enough to look after yourself for an hour or so, aren't you?" she said, pouting into a compact mirror, swiping on a fresh layer of lipstick.

"Where are you going?" I asked.

"To see a friend of my aunt. We've stayed in touch since she died. I said I'd call in if ever I made it to Glasgow. I won't be long, an hour or so. Besides, you'd only be bored if you came."

Before she left, she surprised me with question I certainly didn't expect.

"What will you do after you leave school, Tom?"

I shrugged.

"You're the brightest boy on the island. I think you should consider coming here, to Glasgow, or Edinburgh, to study. You'll have to take university entrance examinations. I'll talk to the headmaster when we get back. Think about it. We don't have to make a decision yet. But when we get back, we'll discuss it further," she said, and then, getting to her feet, added, "and so think about it. I'll meet you in two hours in the foyer of the gallery."

Then she kissed my forehead and left.

As I drank my tea, I thought, I hoped, that perhaps she'd brought me to Glasgow to see how I liked life away from the island, a dry run, to see how I might cope in a city without her there to guide me.

Our lives had changed so much since Father's death. Now free of his terrible roar, she listened to music and hummed. She picked pretty flowers in the glen and put them in vases around our home. She was relaxed. She was happy. Now, when she smiled, she meant it.

And she was certainly busier, constantly occupied, if not attending to chores at home, then taking long walks, often alone. And like me, she had secrets. That visit to Thomas still rankled. She never did mention it again. But, as long as she knew nothing about my visits to see him, life was good. And that's how it would remain. She was happy, that was all that mattered.

A man wearing a uniform with a dense, impressive moustache smiled as I entered the gallery. A trace of polish from freshly-waxed floors hung in the air, and creaking underfoot, the ancient wooden floorboards glistened.

In the first room I entered, a couple of well-dressed women strolling arm-in-arm and wearing stylish hats whispered to each other. A very tall man sporting a green beret, accompanied by a small, well-behaved dog, sat patiently at his feet as he studied individual paintings.

As I wandered through the galleries, I occasionally stopped, noting down details of various paintings—artists' names, dates, the paintings' most striking features—to discuss them with Thomas on my return.

The most impressive painting I saw that afternoon was of my favourite poet, Robert Burns, by Scottish artist Alexander Nasmyth. Most elegant in a silk cravat, he looked every part the poet we Scots revere, our nation's poet.

I visited each room twice, then waited for Mother on a bench in the foyer. As I was looking back through my notes, she suddenly rushed in shaking her umbrella and sat down beside me, a wide smile making her face glow.

"Now, I hope you enjoyed the gallery," she said. "But now, I have a real treat for you. And for me too. I've bought tickets for the pictures, so come on, or we'll miss the beginning," she said, pulling me by the sleeve out into the rain.

I'd read about the cinema; I'd seen photos of films on screens in books, but to be suddenly on the brink of seeing a moving image on screen for the first time, the excitement I felt is impossible to describe.

And she had tickets for arguably the greatest Hollywood musical extravaganza of all time, *Singin' in the Rain*. Gene Kelly, Jean Hagen and Debbie Reynolds. The most famous stars in the world, dancing, leaping, shimmying, singing such unforgettable songs—*Singin' in the Rain*—*You Were Meant for Me*— *Make 'Em Laugh*—*Broadway Melody* and *All I Do is Dream of You*.

When the film finished, we stumbled out of the theatre into the street still under its spell. Evident from the glow on her face, the shocked wonderment coursing through me was clearly having the same effect on Mother. We rushed directly to a record shop where she bought the soundtrack. When I reminded her that we didn't have a gramophone, her reply was short and simple. Very soon, we would.

The following day, we returned to the island. Alone on deck wrapped in sea mist, I was thinking of Glasgow. The galleries, the museums. *Singin' in the Rain.*

When the island appeared, it looked different, much smaller. A bittersweet sensation shuddered through me. My skin still tingled for the city. I'd felt its pull. I'd glimpsed my future.

Eager to see Thomas, I dropped my bag off at home and rushed to the cottage. I wanted to tell him everything about my Glasgow adventure—the zoo, the gallery, but especially going to the pictures and seeing *Singing' in the Rain*. How they danced, sang, fell in love. All in colour.

He laughed out loud as I attempted dance steps from the film, smiling when I told him Mother had bought the soundtrack though we didn't have a gramophone. His face grew dark as I described the zoo, about the conditions in which the animals were kept, but he smiled again when I told him of the beautiful little black girl.

We also talked about the paintings in the art gallery. And the crowds, and how, amid all this excitement, Mother had even talked of me leaving the island to study in Glasgow or Edinburgh.

He reminded me that I'd be going nowhere if I didn't pass the entrance examination, and our discussion swiftly shifted to my progress with *Wealth of Nations.*

While questions on Smith, or his work, were unlikely to arise explicitly in the examination, examiners looked favourably on responses that referred to sources such as Smith's to support a student's own ideas.

I was about half way through and had many questions concerning complex concepts difficult to understand. For an hour or so that day, and in each subsequent meeting until Christmas when I finally finished Smith's impressive *magnum opus*, we discussed its merits, each meeting serving to clarify any grey areas in my understanding. And for Christmas that year, Thomas insisted I keep his copy.

We began the New Year with the witty and wonderful poetry of Robert Burns. Thomas insisted I read aloud, *O' Once I Love'd*, a lament on finding love only to see it slip away. I stood in the middle of room declaring, "*O once I lov'd a bonnie lass/An' aye I love her still*," thinking of the girl he once loved, now, long, long gone.

He clapped when I finished, then asked me to look at another poem, on a page near the end of the book. I flipped through the pages and we both laughed out loud when I found 'Tam o' Shanter', a narrative poem, not about a hat, but about a man named Tam who luckily escapes the fatal clutches of wicked witches. As I read it, I thought back to a stormy day many years ago and chasing my own tam o' shanter through unfamiliar fields that I now knew so well.

Literary analysis featured heavily in the examination. As such, the purpose of these recitals was for me to understand how to analyse unfamiliar poems or prose passages. As I read, to check my understanding of content and how the writer used language to convey his concerns, Thomas frequently stopped me mid-stanza to ask questions and discuss tone, structure, or other literary techniques employed by the writer. Above all, he stressed, I had to understand the poem or passage before confidently critiquing it. In short, I was to be the expert; did I think it any good?

Gradually, he set me tasks with a greater degree of difficulty. When he handed me a list of poems by Romantic poets—Blake, Wordsworth, Shelley and Byron, I enjoyed teasing out meaning lingering within the subtext. But occasionally, a poem proved so abstract, it left me completely stumped. I complained, assuring Thomas there could be little value in poetry with such abstract meaning. But he knew exactly what he was doing, reminding me time and again that the study of literature, or any other discipline that provided a strategic academic challenge, required a rigorous academic approach. It was for me to find and develop strategies to unlock meaning. I had to read with a critical eye. I had to develop techniques, break sections into smaller parts, read difficult sections numerous times. In short, when critiquing literary works, I had to know the author's work well before adding my voice, my rationale, I was to be perceptive. Perception earned marks.

Mother's small collection of books was growing almost weekly. I often returned from school to find her reading a new book neighbours often brought her after visiting the mainland. They knew of her passion for reading, and a kind neighbour had even built a bookshelf stretching along the entire length of our sitting room which, slowly, was beginning to resemble Thomas'.

On Saturdays, after lunch, we walked on the beach then spent the remainder of the day at home reading and listening to music.

We rarely received visitors on weekends, but one Saturday afternoon, just as we were leaving for the beach, there was a knock at the door.

Over tea, Mr Cruikshank, the headmaster, informed us of the purpose of his visit. To assess my suitability to take the university entrance examination.

Before starting his assessment, he warned that such an ambitious endeavour required laborious preparation, then proceeded to test me with a series of questions, mainly on literature.

Supporting my ideas with citations from works by Orwell, Hemingway and Yeats, and drawing on discussions I'd had with Thomas, I surprised both Mother and the headmaster with my responses. The final question, unrelated to literature, to do with self-sustainability of Scottish islands, permitted me to demonstrate my familiarity with Smith's

Wealth of Nations, and I launched enthusiastically into a lengthy explanation of cooperative practices within low-yielding agricultural economies.

When the headmaster interrupted my response, bringing the interview to an abrupt close, in the silence that followed, I thought I'd fallen at this first hurdle.

As he looked around the room, at the books lining the new shelves, I trembled, readying myself to rush off to my room if he considered me an unsuitable candidate.

He finished his tea, drew in a deep breath and cleared his throat. Based on school reports, and my thorough responses that afternoon, all seemed in order. He'd begin preparatory administrative procedures for me to sit the examination immediately.

Mother accompanied him to the door, where he paused. Turning, he looked at me, holding me with a firm gaze. I thought he might have changed his mind. But then, briefly, he warned me again about the need to work hard, then left.

Mother closed the door, ran to me, and throwing her arms around me, kissed my head, lifted me up and swung me round. What for so long had been, more or less, simply a possibility, had now become a reality.

That final year on the island yielded so many memorable events—the headmaster's visit, my first trip to the mainland, however, my most treasured memory occurred one afternoon a few days after Mr Cruikshank's interview, just as I arrived home from school.

Almost exclusively, Mother listened to classical music on the wireless. But the melody in our home that afternoon was decidedly lighter, more contemporary. And familiar.

I rushed in to catch her stomping around the house to Gene Kelly's *Singin' in in the Rain*. Her face flushed, sweat glistening on her forehead, she froze when she saw me. In the corner of the room, a shiny new gramophone, the title track to *Singin' in in the Rain* blaring from it. Suddenly, she rushed forward, grabbed hold of me, swung me around, and together, we tramped around the house, stamping in imaginary puddles, growing delightfully dizzy as we laughed.

The happiest moment of my life.

11

Independent of each other, and in their own way, Mother, Thomas and, to the best of his ability, my schoolteacher, steered me towards what we all hoped would be a successful outcome in the university examination. With an almost religious devotion, I studied, reading late into the night and rising early, two hours before school, to read more.

And yet, I still worried I wasn't doing enough. Never far away, dark thoughts about failing constantly lurked. I wouldn't know enough. I'd open the question paper and draw a blank. On some days, such concerns grew so heavy I convinced myself I didn't know anything, all my efforts pointless. Failure was inevitable.

At school, one morning, the headmaster interrupted a lesson and asked me to accompany him to his office. I thought, perhaps, there was a problem with my taking the examination. With such thoughts constantly flashing through me, it would have been a relief. But his summons was brief, only adding to the pressure I already felt, a simple reminder that my performance on the examination would, in no small way, reflect his as headmaster of the school.

Each morning, from either the wireless or gramophone, I woke to the sound of music. I especially recall Mother's favourite, cantatas by Ivor Stravinsky. Beautiful, haunting voices, weaved so soothingly into melodies, I would lay awake listening to her happily humming along, precious, but fleeting moments that dissolved as my mind wandered to thoughts of the day ahead, and irrational speculation about failing the examination suddenly returned.

I woke one Saturday in such low spirits, truly convinced that everything would go wrong, that I'd fail the examination miserably, and though Mother had already served breakfast, I slipped quietly out and ran to the cliffs.

When I heard again the familiar sound of bickering puffins, short snarls followed by delightful little 'laughs', and saw the thousands upon thousands of birds soaring in and out over the big blue Atlantic, a simply wondrous sight, a miraculous moment of clarity suddenly descended. If I failed, if I had to remain on this island surrounded by such extraordinary beauty, then, so be it. I could do no more than I was doing. I was working as hard as I could. If I had to stay, I'd continue seeing Thomas, reading, listening to music with him, and continue taking walks with Mother. Such simple things I loved to do.

Mother recognised the pressure I was under, and after lunch that afternoon, she asked me to accompany her on a long walk. As we strolled along the beach, she held my hand and told me how proud she was of me, impressed with such dedication to my studies.

"How far that little candle throws its beams," she said, a reference to Shakespeare's *Merchant of Venice*. I understood the metaphor, that my journey, my ordeal, was nearly over, and that in these dark and difficult moments of frustration, I shouldn't lose sight of my objective. I was to keep going.

Our discussion of Shakespeare continued as we walked. His life, his plays, what stirred his characters. We agreed Lear was naïve, foolish, and that with the exception of Cordelia, his daughters got what they deserved. As did the Macbeths.

Our views on Shylock differed however. I thought him an evil wretch whose relentless greed led to his demise. But Mother would have none of it, conceding he was, indeed, a devilish antagonist, but heroic, his views on self-serving Christians not only justified, but valiant, noble even. That by challenging the double standards of those cruel, hypocritical Christians, Shylock championed the rights of the downtrodden. A lone voice, one man, challenging base discrimination against all the odds, his efforts to free himself of cruel entrapment deserving of praise, not criticism, and only through trickery and corrupt deception by a twisted, unmerciful establishment did he lose everything—his wealth, his faith and, probably most importantly, his dignity.

Our discussion shifted to America. To the rights of its citizens, its Constitution, about how that nation proclaimed democratic values for 'all' while tolerating segregation. Smith frequently mentioned America in *Wealth of Nations*, yet my enduring memory of how that country treated its people was from a newspaper article I read with Thomas, detailing the events of a public lynching, a ritual slaughter, much like a bullfight. Accompanying the article, a disturbing photograph of a burning corpse, of a black man, hanging limply from a tree as a baying mob looked at the camera, smiling.

Mother described America as a 'young experiment in democracy', still struggling with civil rights, like segregation, especially in southern states where treatment of black people was clearly still barbaric. She added that as a 'work in progress', America would, hopefully, one day, provide all of its citizens with the rights promised in its Constitution.

Thomas said such struggles for rights are well documented throughout history, and that when people united, got together and protested, worked together, they limited the influence of unjust governments and tyrannical monarchies, thus improving the lives of many. He cited a relatively recent example, the French Revolution, which, despite much bloodshed, resulted in new laws protecting citizens' rights, much like those set out in the American Constitution.

Mother's keen interest in literature and music pleased me. I hoped that, in some small way, such interests would cushion the blow of my departure and help her cope with the monotony of island life if I passed the examination and left for university.

And one day, I discovered her interests didn't solely include highbrow tastes such as Schuman and Shakespeare. Returning from school one afternoon I found her curled up on the couch cradling a mug of tea, enthralled with a BBC radio play, *Mrs Dale's Diary*. Set in London, the play explores the life of a woman, Mrs Dale, a doctor's wife, and how she manages events in her own hectic life as she struggles with the wily ways of her own errant family members, the play revolving around the type of sinful behaviour the minister claimed was part and parcel of mainland living—secret marriages, unexpected births, sudden departures, shocking infidelity—the type of scandal that would never darken the door of an island widow. Schuman, Shakespeare, Mrs Dale. Whatever form of entertainment made her happy after my departure made me happy. About a month before the examination, my discussions with Thomas ceased. My focus, from that point on: examination practice. Without interruption. Much to his bewilderment, rather than sleeping below my desk as I worked, as he usually did, Mot was held prisoner in the studio for a couple of hours, released only when I finished the practice essay.

Thomas marked my essays overnight, and the following day, we discussed the merits of these responses, always looking for ways in which they might be improved. Careless errors in spelling and grammar irritated examiners and earned me a mild scolding. But when he complimented me, on an original idea, or a well-constructed sentence, smiling and nodding, a warm rush flooded through me, filling me with confidence, making me want to work harder.

A week before the examination, I arrived home to see Mother sitting at the kitchen table, a worried look on her face, one I had seen often when Father was alive. Something was wrong. I breathed a sigh of relief when she pointed to a letter from the university propped up against the sugar bowl.

She opened it, her hands trembling as she read aloud procedural instructions for the day of the examination. Time, place, what I needed to bring, and as I listened, I felt what can only be described as a moment of liberation. The end was in sight.

On the morning of the examination, I woke early and lay staring at the ceiling, daydreaming about what questions might come up. Despite music drifting into my room, I heard whispered voices coming from the kitchen. I dressed quickly but found Mother alone, standing at the kitchen sink, holding a small package.

"Here," she said, handing it to me, "it will bring you luck."

Sitting at the kitchen table, I carefully removed the wrapping to find a long black box, the word Sheaffer embossed in gold on the lid. Inside, the most beautiful, gleaming fountain pen. I loaded it with ink, signed my name and wrote the date on a scrap of paper, the nib, like a blade on ice, gliding smoothly across the paper. I assured her that with such a wonderful pen, I'd pass the examination easily.

"We'll have a picnic afterwards. To celebrate. Up on the cliffs. We can watch the puffins," she said. "It's going to be a beautiful day."

The headmaster, looking very anxious, was waiting for us at the school gate. He bid Mother a polite good morning then led me to his office where he sat me before a small desk directly in front of his. On a small blackboard leaning against the wall behind his desk, he had scribbled, in chalk, the start and finish times of the examination.

He coughed gently, then ceremoniously read aloud lengthy instructions on how the examination would be conducted. Once he'd finished, he stepped forward holding a large brown envelope. Opening it slowly, he pulled from it the question booklet, glancing briefly at the questions. Then, placing it on the desk in front of me, he retreated to his chair behind his desk, and for the next three hours, I worked industriously, occasionally looking up at the clock above the headmaster's desk to see him smoking one cigarette after another, watching me from within a cloud of blue smoke. Only many years later did I learn from an island elder that that was the only official examination Mr Cruikshank had ever overseen, and for years long after I'd left the island, he spoke of me in glowing terms.

He rang a bell to signal the end of the examination. I'd finished four essays, read back through each, and made corrections where necessary.

After three hours in a stuffy room, the cool air of the playground was such welcome relief. A picnic basket at her side, Mother was waiting patiently on a small bench near the gate. When I called, she ran to me, wrapping me in her arms.

On our way to the cliffs, I told her I found the most challenging questions those on literature. One required analysis of a passage from Alexander Pope's *Rape of the Lock*. I knew the poem well, had discussed it with Thomas at length, and so, released a muted whisper of delight when I saw it which prompted the headmaster to sternly remind me that the examination was to be conducted in absolute silence.

I answered the question confidently, focusing on the mock-heroic nature of the poem, what I hoped the examiners were looking for. And strangely, as I summarised my responses on the examination, I could feel the anxiety, the worry, slowly slipping from me, my body growing lighter. It was finally over. I could relax. I could breathe again.

The sun was high in a cloudless sky when we reached the cliffs. Mother, humming happily, prepared the picnic, patting flat then neatly arranging the contents of the basket on the picnic blanket. In a pensive mood, I sat near the cliff edge looking out at the vast Atlantic sky.

Hundreds and thousands of puffins, twisting and turning, soared between the cliffs and the sea. What simple lives they led.

With the examination behind me, change lay ahead; I was about to enter unchartered regions. After months of hard, unrelenting slog, now without a care in the world, my body tingled. Finally, I felt free. Since Father's death, Mother had made great sacrifices for me. I often wondered how the changes about to take place in my life would disrupt hers. Only a year or so later, in my second year of university, well on my way to successfully making my own way in the world, did I learn that such concern was unnecessary, and 'exactly' how shrewd and resourceful she really was.

An example of such resourcefulness lay spread across the blanket that afternoon, products so hard to come by, luxuries still rationed—butter, milk, boiled eggs, canned meat, cheese, sugar and Scottish salmon, a delicacy normally reserved for Christmas.

As we ate, I detailed my responses to other questions on the examination. One, clearly of the moment, enquired how best a country might recover after a calamitous event like war.

I proposed that all governments had a moral obligation to ensure secure futures for all citizens. Since the poor sacrificed most during war, they needed the most help. Countries should prioritise the rights of the working classes, educate them about their rights, give them a stake in their country, foster in them renewed feelings of national pride. By creating a jobs programmes for them to rebuild the country, they would feel a genuine sense of ownership, instilling in them the importance of their efforts in creating a bright future for all citizens of the nation. Newly-enshrined labour statutes, much like the tenets of the American Constitution, should protect these jobs, guaranteeing all citizens good and decent lives.

Such utopian ideals appeared to impress Mother who, with little more to add, smiled. Then, stretching out across the blanket, she took up her book and began to read. I returned to the cliff edge where I lay on my back looking up into an enormous blue sky, at tiny black and white specks whirling and swirling as if in celebration, thousands upon thousands of puffins, more than I'd ever seen before.

When I heard a familiar yap, I glanced over at Mother sleeping soundly, her book resting on her stomach. Looking out over the cliff edge down to the beach below, I saw Thomas on his horse, Mot squirming in his arms. I wanted to rush down the cliff path and tell him about the examination, but Mother suddenly sprang to her feet and asked me to help pack things away.

Mot barked as I approached Thomas' cottage later that afternoon. The door opened and he scampered out, followed by Thomas who greeted me with a warm embrace. Over tea, he listened carefully, occasionally nodding as I provided details about the examination. He declared how proud he was of me, a declaration he had used from time to time over the years, but this time, perhaps because I'd finally achieved something, accomplished something, I really did feel proud of my efforts. We listened to music then went for a short walk on the beach, and as we parted that afternoon, he handed me a small paint pot and asked me to open it. Inside, a pale mottled green marble pebble, similar to the one I gave Mother for her birthday. He said it would bring me luck.

A week after the examination, Mother surprised me with another visit to Glasgow. Three magical days of splendid weather, museums, galleries and wandering the city's streets. Delighting us as much as the first time, we saw *Singin' in the Rain* again.

On my return, I experienced another notable event, probably the most exhilarating yet terrifying of my life.

On the beach one morning with Thomas, he hoisted me up onto his horse. Sitting nervously in the saddle, the horse ambled lazily through the waves at a steady pace. Rather prematurely, I thought the experience pleasant. However, quite unexpectedly, Thomas slapped the beast's buttock, and suddenly, it bolted, galloping down the beach, my arms around its neck holding on for dear life. A lifetime later, on the sound of Thomas' whistle, the creature slowed, resumed a leisurely pace, snorting and shaking its head, as if laughing.

Painting together later that afternoon in his studio, Thomas suddenly burst out laughing. He briefly reminded me of the spectacle on the beach, of how terrified I looked. At first, I wasn't amused, I've never been near a horse since, but thinking of how ridiculous I must have looked, I eventually came around and laughed along with him.

The summer sped by, August arrived. Days were growing shorter and I could feel my life as an islander drawing to a close. Before me, looming large, a separation I didn't feel ready for, one I tried to convince myself I no longer desired it. I longed for an extension to these years of golden childhood.

Some nights, I cried myself to sleep, thinking I'd be happier if I failed the examination. I wanted to keep things as they were. Stay on the island, carry on as before.

Results arrived mid-August. I got up to find Mother sitting at the kitchen table, ghostly pale, gazing at the official brown envelope in her hands. Wiping sleep from my eyes, I joined her. She suggested I have breakfast before opening it. But I was impatient.

She handed me the envelope.

In stilted prose, the letter informed me that I'd passed with distinction. The university now awaited my response.

In tears, Mother rushed around the table, and holding me so tightly, I felt her thrashing heart, reminding me of how, in this very spot, she had stood up to Father so many years ago.

Then, quite unexpectedly, she took me by the hand, led me to the door and opened it. Gathered outside, a handful of neighbours released a muted cheer and broke into spontaneous applause. Surprised and mildly embarrassed, I'll never forget the gentle, generous happiness on their faces.

12

Thomas greeted me with a big, welcoming smile. As always, Mot yelped and jumped, curling himself into the contours of my lap as I slumped onto the sofa.

Sitting for the last time in a room now so familiar, the books themselves like friends, I felt an overwhelming sorrow. Years of cherished childhood joy, stirring memories I'd carry with me always, now at an end. It was time to say goodbye.

Thomas brought in the tea, smiling as he poured, but unable to disguise a heavy sigh. Both of us knew this day was different, unlike the untroubled, halcyon days we'd enjoyed over the years.

As the tea splashed into the cups, he joked, suggesting we get to work. I burst into tears.

He sat beside me and put his arm around my shoulder, Mot snuggling in between us licking tears from my chin.

"Tom," he said, a tremor in his whisper. "It's time for the rest of your life to begin. You're no longer a boy; it's time to make your way in the world. Meet people, see places, learn about life. We've had these long years together, happy years, certainly the happiest of my life. Now, it's time for you to experience more of the world, and you can only do that alone, son. The island will always be here. Besides," he said, resting his head on my shoulder, "spare a thought for the puffin chicks nudged out of their nests in just a matter of weeks."

Kind words, but I simply didn't feel ready, I still felt very much the child. The thought of going alone in the world weighed so heavily in me.

In the days and weeks leading to this moment, alone on the beach, or up on the cliffs, I'd been thinking of what I'd say, what words I'd use to thank him for all he'd done for me. But I had none. Just childish tears. I dreaded not having him, or Mother, in my life. I was deserting them. Condemning them both to lives of silent loneliness.

We hugged our goodbyes. He whispered he'd come and see me in Edinburgh. Mot barked. I picked him up and let him lick my face, telling him that I'd miss him and that he should come to the mainland too. Thomas nodded.

I arrived home exhausted. Mother was sitting on my bed. By the door, my suitcase. I sat beside her, she took my hand in hers, both of us fighting back tears. She echoed, more or less, what Thomas had said, that I had the rest of my life to live, the time had come for me to go out and live it.

That night, that awful last night, I barely slept. Still awake as the sun rose, I secretly hoped the day might defy natural law, the sun sink back into the horizon and undo time, rewind, give me back my childhood.

It came time to leave. Case in hand, I took one last look around my home.

Mother opened the door, and as they had on the morning I received my results, islanders had gathered outside to see me off.

I stepped out and the hum faded. I looked around at faces I knew so well, some of which I was seeing for the last time that morning.

Mr Cruikshank, the headmaster, stepped forward, shook my hand, bowed his head, and handed me a volume of poems by Alexander Pope. Then others followed, one by one approaching, saying little, a simple 'good luck' or 'be safe', each presenting me with a gift, most handmade, tokens from the island itself. A small vial of sand. Tiny pebbles from the beach. Keepsakes that would bring me luck.

The most precious gift, however, came from a small, shy boy. Though certain I'd not seen him before, his pretty face looked familiar. Perhaps three or four, he was no higher than my waist. Reluctant to step forward, he looked up at his mother who nodded encouragement, pushing him gently towards me.

I dropped to my haunches, smiled and beckoned him to me. In his tiny hands, a frame. With his head bowed, he stretched out his arm, passed it to me then rushed back to his mother, this sweet and gentle act of generosity prompting the gathering to release a long 'aaaaaaaah'.

I glanced down at the frame to see a simple painting of a puffin. The small, orange splotches for the beak and feet, a small white blob on the chest, instantly reminding me of the puffin I'd painted on the day I met Thomas. Looking up, I saw the boy buried within the folds of his mother's dress, and with tears in my eyes, as I whispered her my appreciation, only then did I recognise Annabel, the girl from school, the girl I loved all those years ago.

On the ferry to the mainland, I was inconsolable. What I'd always thought would be a day of celebration, liberation, the happiest of my life, felt like the worst, like a custodial sentence.

To lift my spirits, Mother tried offering words of reassurance, but nothing she said pierced me.

The ferry docked and we caught the bus to Edinburgh.

My home for the next few years was a small terraced house a short walk from the city centre. Miss Campbell shared the house with her friend, Miss Fischer, two women Mother knew well. Overjoyed at our arrival, they warmly welcomed us, both women embracing Mother and shaking my hand before leading us into the sitting room.

On a small round table covered in a beautifully embroidered tablecloth of fine lace, an assortment of tea and cakes. The two women were kind, softly spoken, attentive. They asked me about my studies, and told me about Mother's aunt who had lived with them before returning to the island to take care of her.

After half an hour or so, Miss Campbell showed us to my room. It was nicer than expected, a crackling coal fire making it surprisingly warm and welcoming. In the window alcove looking out onto the street, a study desk with a lamp, and above the fire on the mantelpiece, a photograph, women on a beach, young, attractive, smiling at the camera. Mother picked it up and pointed to one of the women, her aunt, the last occupant of the room.

I sat on the bed and watched Mother unpack my suitcase. As she hung my shirts in a large wardrobe and arranged the rest of my clothes neatly in the chest of drawers, she reminded me of my responsibilities whilst living with these women. To be kind and respectful. To follow rules. To study hard.

She put the empty suitcase under the bed, puffed out the pillow and looked around to check all was in order then we returned to the sitting room where the women had made a fresh pot of tea.

It came time for Mother to leave.

That slow and silent walk to the train station still makes me shudder when I think about it.

Standing on the platform, Mother informed me she would be spending the next few days in Glasgow. She had 'important things to do'. I suspect she didn't want to be too far away as I settled into city life.

Then, taking me in her arms, she held me firmly, kissed my forehead and again reminded me of the importance to work hard, avoid alcohol and try not to smoke. I promised to write at least once a week.

She boarded the train, and as it pulled away, I waved what felt like a final farewell, and as it disappeared, I had the strangest, most unsettling feeling. That I would never see her again.

And suddenly, I felt so lost.

During those first few days at university, I felt like an intruder. I tried my best to blend in, slipping quickly into a daily routine, attending lectures in the morning, then, after lunch, wandering the university's sprawling campus observing fellow students, fascinated by their casual, youthful optimism.

I expected most students to be like me, young, Scottish, coming from a similar background to mine, small obscure backwaters scattered throughout the country. But with a student body surprisingly diverse, I quickly grew accustomed to the sound of foreign accents. Many students had even attended fee-paying public schools in England. Others, older, men and women, were finishing their studies after serving in the forces, such a mingling giving the city an exciting cosmopolitan air.

Heeding Mother's advice, I remained focused on my studies, waking each morning excited by the day ahead, inspiring lectures by inspiring professors, ingenious men who, like Thomas, nourished hungry, young minds with robust debate and worldly wisdom.

The distractions I suspect Mother had referred to, pretty girls, were everywhere in the city. I didn't mention this most agreeable aspect of university life in letters I wrote most afternoons to both Thomas and Mother. Instead, from a small city centre cafe, I assured them I was settling in well, and that Miss Fischer and Miss Campbell, both angels, were feeding me very well. Lectures were stimulating, the people (many foreign) were interesting, friendly, and the city was constantly moving. But I missed home.

On days I received a letter, from either Mother or Thomas, it felt like my birthday. I read it first during the break between lectures, then again that afternoon in the cafe. When two letters arrived on the same day, it felt like Christmas. One day in particular when this happened has since become one of the most memorable days of my life...

I was running late, had just closed the door behind me when I ran into the postman on the doorstep. He handed me two letters, one from Mother, the other from Thomas. I tucked them into my jacket pocket, hurried off, and in the break between lectures, read them in the university canteen.

Mother was doing well, taking long walks along the cliffs in fine weather, sometimes taking the cliff path down to the beach to collect small rocks she had added to my collection. The neighbour had put up another shelf in the sitting room, for books she had bought on trips to Glasgow. Though always tempted to come and see me, for now, while

I settled in, I needed no distractions, not even a visit from her. I was to remain focused on my studies.

I often wondered if she saw Thomas again. In his letters, he recommended places to visit. Theatres, teashops, public libraries. He also said I should visit Glasgow, a vibrant city somewhat more 'Scottish' than Edinburgh. Happy that university was living up to expectations, he often referred to his wise words in our last meeting, repeating the importance of 'making my own way in the world', and 'to find what was waiting for me'. I always thought he'd used these words to cushion the blow of our impending separation, but just as I was returning his letter to the envelope, his words proved timely when, quite expectedly, I felt a tap on my shoulder.

"Excuse me, is this seat free?" she said, lowering herself into the seat opposite. "You're in my History of Art lecture. My name's Lucia," she added, her beautiful smile captivating me instantly.

I told her my name and felt the sides of my neck grow warm. When she discovered I was an islander, she grew visibly excited, assaulting me with a barrage of questions about island life, until then an experience I'd considered entirely unremarkable.

She was half-Italian, but wholly stunning. In that first encounter, she did most of the talking, providing me with an impromptu lesson on both Scottish and European history.

She was an offshoot of the most recent Italian diaspora to settle in Scotland. In fact, modern-day Italy didn't exist when the first wave of Italians, Romans, arrived in AD 71, marauding imperialists who developed a semblance of Scotland's first infrastructure, roads on which they hoped to suppress frequent Celtic rebellion. And they built things, the most notable still with us fourteen hundred years after their departure, two indelible landmarks, two walls, Hadrian's and Antonine's.

Many Italians had come more recently, early in the century during World War I, mainly to Glasgow, to work in the shipyards. Lucia, however, had sprung from an even more recent arrival, a jolly Sicilian, fleeing poverty in his homeland in the late 1920s. Her father, Luigi, had no intention of staying. He had come simply to earn enough money to return to his beloved island where he had intended to build a small house in the country, meet a beautiful girl, have lots of children and live a long and splendid life.

However, he soon tired of backbreaking labour of shipyard work, and as a man of enterprise, invested his meagre savings into a small, derelict city centre cafe which, after refurbishment, became a popular hangout for Glasgow's teens. An excellent cook, he worked tirelessly to make his business a success, his plans of returning to the balmy climes of Sicily crumbling on the day he first glimpsed Lucia's mother, Kathleen, coming into the cafe one morning looking for a job.

Her flowing red hair and soft alabaster skin convinced Luigi immediately of her talents, so first, he gave her a job, then three months later, a ring.

With Kathleen at his side, and as supplies became more available, they opened the first Italian restaurant in Glasgow, such an instant success that Luigi invited his twin brother to join him, and they opened two more. Lucia and I began to meet regularly. By spring of that first year, we'd become inseparable. But meeting a girl, falling in love, the distraction that Mother had mentioned, at first worried me too. I thought about Lucia constantly, even during lectures, and worried my studies would suffer. In reality, however, from discussions we had together, and within a small circle of friends, I developed a broader understanding of the world and the people in it which, ultimately, enlightened rather than hindered my academic progress.

At first, I was reluctant to meet her family. But she proved persuasive, constantly singing their praises and her hometown, Glasgow.

I remember entering the kitchen of her family home, and seeing her parents for the first time. Her mother, at the kitchen table reading a newspaper, humming along to music from the wireless. Her father, up to his elbows in flour, kneading dough for bread. He worked most days, but with

Lucia coming home, he'd left the restaurants in the capable hands of his brother.

When they saw Lucia, their faces lit up, rushing over to her, embracing her, kissing her forehead. They greeted me with equally beautiful smiles, warm handshakes, assuring me I was most welcome, my anxiety about measuring up quickly dissolving. Her mother made tea and her father, returning to his dough, wanted to hear about life growing up on a remote Scottish island.

During lunch, the doorbell rang several times, each time Luigi springing up to usher in neighbours, the kitchen soon full of laughter.

At one point he called for quiet, raised a glass, and welcomed me to the fold, winking at his wife as he announced that, like him, Lucia's boyfriend was an islander, and as such, he and I shared a bond, we were special, and the women in our lives, his wife and daughter, were lucky to have us. Everyone laughed, Lucia lovingly rebuking him, reminding him that as Britons, we were all islanders.

Later that afternoon I glanced across the table. Lucia smiled at me, and in that moment, I knew it was time to tell Mother and Thomas I was in love.

Early on in our relationship, I had told Lucia about my childhood, leaving no shameful detail out. Of Father, a cruel and angry man, and of his absurd death. Of Mother, reading to me in secret. My secret visits to see Thomas. She commented that I'd had many secrets as a boy. She also thought Mother a saint and Thomas an impressive man of great stature. She wanted to meet them.

I drafted so many letters, in each struggling to find the words to describe Lucia, now so central to my life. Growing frustrated, I finally sent two, one to Mother the other to Thomas. Containing few words, I simply said that I'd met a girl and I'd be bringing her home this summer.

Five days later, again, two letters arrived on the same day. Both Mother and Thomas expressed genuine excitement at seeing me, and very much looking forward to meeting Lucia.

13

The ferry docked. Mother ran to me, tears streaming down her face. She kissed me, said I'd grown, and as if meeting an old friend, hugged Lucia, kissing her on both cheeks.

She looked different. Like the beautiful young woman I remember seeing on the day she went with Father to the island assembly, the day I returned to see Thomas.

After a long lunch of fine Scottish salmon and lively discussion, she suggested I take Lucia to the cliffs.

As we wandered along lanes I knew so well, childhood memories came flooding back, and that first glimpse of the sea, a deep rich turquoise, took my breath away. When I heard the familiar chatter of puffins, I seized Lucia's hand and we ran the last hundred feet to the cliff edge to see thousands, perhaps millions of tiny puffins soaring across the sky.

Sitting on the soft grass close to the cliff edge, Lucia described the view as magical. I had to agree. Though I'd spent my childhood looking out at this magnificent horizon stretching across that mighty ocean, for the first time I felt proud to be born in a place of such supreme beauty.

I pointed to the stretch of beach where I'd first seen Thomas on horseback galloping along the shore and told Lucia again of that magical moment I first saw him, almost a divine experience, his arrival in my life when I most needed it.

Eager to meet the outcast responsible for guiding me to her, hand in hand, we took the cliff path down to the beach.

As we approached the cottage, I thought of Mother, looking so well, happy, young, beautiful. Of being back home, up on the cliffs with the puffins, and of Thomas, a man who had so selflessly given me so much, who had shown me how to find happiness, put me on the path to living a good and decent life. But above all, inadvertently, he'd guided me to Lucia, the most wonderful gift of all.

When I saw the cottage, about to be once more in the presence of this most wonderful of men, I remembered how I felt the day I returned to see him. Nervous, unsure, full of trepidation. Similar feelings rushed through me, but this time, fused with such profound gratitude. And as thoughts of how he had gently guided me, of his gentle nature, of what he himself had to sacrifice in his own life, I had to stop, take deep breaths, and steady myself.

But then I heard the most wonderful sound, that familiar yelp, and suddenly, saw Mot sprinting along the path towards us, whining as he leapt into my arms, panting wildly, licking my face, his little tail wagging so excitedly.

In his apron smeared with paint, Thomas was waiting at the door, smiling. He shook Lucia's hand and as he hugged me, tears rolled down my face.

"Son, son, son! What's with all these tears! These are happy days, come on in. I've made tea," he said, leaving us in the sitting room and disappearing momentarily to put the finishing touches to the cake he'd made especially.

Being back in the room where, in many ways, life for me began, is difficult to describe. But sat on the couch stroking Mot, watching Lucia circle the room browsing the books was almost magical.

Over tea we told Thomas all about our exciting lives at university. He knew some of Lucia's art professors, one of them very well, an old and very good friend who had spent a summer on the island with Thomas painting, many of those paintings now in his studio. Lucia shifted excitedly when he mentioned his studio.

We finished our tea and Thomas took us through, Lucia's face lighting up when she saw the hundreds of paintings, drifting slowly around the studio, pausing as she inspected individual paintings.

"Who painted this?" she asked, looking up at a painting of the cliffs Thomas had been working on the day I met him.

"Oh, that's the cliffs, I…" Thomas began.

"No. The small one next to it. The puffin," she said, staring at the smaller canvas next to Thomas'.

"Lucia," Thomas said, smiling at me. "This is one of my favourites. Let's just say a good and decent man painted this. Clearly, a man of great skill. You see how well he's blended in those colours? Here," he said, removing it from its hook and gazing at it. "A gift, from one artist to another," he added, wrapping it in hessian sacking and handing it to a slightly embarrassed Lucia.

Seeing again the puffin I'd begun the day I met him brought on more tears, and I had to excuse myself.

Before leaving, we drank more tea and listened to the soprano, Mary Gardner, whose angelic voice I now knew so well. We told Thomas about our plans to cross another frontier that summer, on this occasion, the border between Scotland and England. We were going to London. Thomas scribbled down places of interest he recommended we visit, adding that he'd be on the mainland soon, in Glasgow, for business. He'd see us then.

With my painting tucked under her arm, Lucia and I walked back along the beach. She declared Thomas an impressive man. An 'artist and intellectual' more 'Glasgow, Berlin or Paris' than small island. In me, she saw many of his qualities, adding that a man with such refined tastes, a curious mind, and quite clearly such a caring nature, would make a fine husband. I shivered with pride.

Then, strangely, she said that I had his eyes.

The distress I thought I'd feel on leaving the island, leaving Mother, was somewhat alleviated by her telling me she was planning another trip to Glasgow soon. As we walked to the harbour, she told me she thought Lucia beautiful, a woman of character who clearly made me happy. I was to bring her back soon, adding that when we met in Glasgow, she wanted to hear all about London. And we were to send her a postcard of the river Thames.

Thomas knew London well. Reluctantly, he called it possibly the greatest city on earth. Its only drawback, he joked, the Sassenachs who lived in it. On the train south, we studied the list of places he'd recommended we visit. In addition to the names of a few lively pubs, there was the theatre, opera, walks by the Thames, galleries, museums, all of which we spent the week visiting.

On our last day, as we wandered the winding alleyways near St Paul's cathedral, we stumbled on Samuel Johnson's House, now a museum.

Thomas had told me about this particular 'Sassenach' visiting our island in the eighteenth century, leaving shortly after arriving, severely critical of its people, and for this reason, I was no great admirer of the man. But after passing a week in a glorious city, *his* city, and wandering through the house in which he had so meticulously laboured to create the dictionary, an extraordinary feat, I couldn't deny my admiration for him.

On the train back to Edinburgh, in a biography written by his good friend, John Boswell, I read for the first time, his now familiar quote in praise of the capital, 'that when a man is tired of London, he is tired of life: for there is in London all that life can afford'. Somewhat reluctantly, both Lucia and I had to agree, and we discussed briefly the possibility of one day living there.

The second year of university proved more demanding. Though my workload increased substantially, I relished the academic challenge. Participation in a number of clubs and societies kept our evenings busy, and we spent most weekends in Glasgow with Lucia's family.

Everything was going so well.

Until that morning in early October when Miss Campbell knocked to inform me the postman was at the door with a letter requiring my signature. As I signed, I recognised Mother's handwriting. Immediately, I felt, I knew, the contents of the letter contained disturbing news and I became unsteady on my feet.

Noting my distress, Miss Campbell took me through to the sitting room and Miss Fischer brought in tea. They offered kind words, said I should open it, reassuring me that 'there's no need to worry'. But the letter contained terrible news, of this I was certain. I had the evidence shaking in my hand, the return address, in Glasgow, not our island home, confirming my worst fears, and despite their best intentions, their gentle words could not deter me from thinking anything but the worst.

I finished the tea, thanked my landladies as best I could for their well-meaning words, and returned to my room in a state of hopeless distress.

The letter trembled in my hand, my heart thumped in my ears and thinking of Mother's frequent visits to the mainland, Glasgow, three times since I'd been in Edinburgh, convinced me she was in grave danger.

Not once had she come to see me, her claims, excuses, of not wanting to interrupt my studies, there to buy books and records to make island life 'more tolerable', now rang hollow. I thought back to our first visit to Glasgow together. Of her leaving me alone in the gallery to see a friend of her 'aunt', and of how weary she looked on her return, a certain sadness in her eyes.

This letter, a confession, contained a truth she could no longer keep hidden from me. She was ill. Terminally ill. Those visits to Glasgow, hospital appointments.

The most perfect mother, sacrificing her happiness in life so I could have mine. In my hand, in this letter, disguised between bouncy, well-meaning words insisting I live a long and happy life, was a terrible word that signalled the end. One word, one solitary, unutterable word about to destroy everything I had. And the moment I opened that letter, the moment I read that word, it would be branded in me forever.

Cancer.

My sorrowful howl brought Miss Campbell and Miss Fischer rushing into my room without knocking. Sitting with me on the bed, again they tried to console me, gently coaxing me to open the letter, insisting that I was needlessly upsetting myself, assuring me that it contained good news.

But how could these caring, gentle women, with caring, gentle words possibly know?

Miss Fischer took the letter and opened it, and then those two dear women left. Looking down at the letter, tears, blurring my vision, fell and stained the paper.

Dear Tom,

No doubt you'll be surprised to receive this letter. Firstly, I want to assure you I am very well and you should NOT be alarmed. My intention was to wait until you had finished university before sending such correspondence, but when you came home this summer with Lucia, such a bright and beautiful girl, it was clear to me that you left a boy and came home a man! Seeing you so happy with Lucia and learning about your ambitious plans for the future, I was and am so thrilled for you both.

Tom, my boy, you always have been and still are central to my life. We've been through some tough times together, now, thankfully, all in the past. And now, you are making your own way in the world, I think it's about time I started to make mine. The reason I send you this letter.

I often think of those afternoons we read and listened to music together, the most wonderful moments of my life. But those days I know will never return. Since your father's passing and you leaving, I have been trying to get on with life. Living on the island my entire life, I have scant knowledge of the world or the people who inhabit it. Like most island girls, I married your father young, about the age you are now. But I married him quickly, within a month of meeting him. I was naïve, I thought I might change his hard exterior, that married life might soften him. We both know that didn't happen. The truth is, I never understood him and he never understood me. And, I know you'll understand when I say I never loved him, and I doubt he ever loved me.

When you were born, he grew even more withdrawn, and as you got older, he made little effort to understand you,

Tom. I have my suspicions why, which I won't go into here, but he was consumed with such anger, anger that made him a sad and terribly troubled man. Sometimes, as you witnessed, for no reason, he would explode. And we bore the brunt of this. And for this, I'm truly sorry. But he was, like most of us islanders, simply a product of where we were born. A place that few escape. But that's all in the past now, and, like you, I'm only interested in the future, a bright and beautiful future.

And so, now to the reason I write this letter. To tell you about my plans for the future, which, I'm sure will come as a surprise.

I'm in good health, still relatively young, and yet, all I've ever known is the island. I now want to explore; I want to experience more in life. Even as a small girl, I dreamt of leaving the island, but first came the war, and then other, unforeseen circumstances which prevented me from doing so. I told you little about my childhood for many reasons. My parents died when I was young, and my aunt, whose room you now occupy, returned from Edinburgh to take care of me. She was a good woman who did her best, always teaching me to get on in life. In my teenage years, I had dreams of leaving the island, which she encouraged, always telling me stories about the excitement of life on the mainland.

I was young and carefree and had every intention of leaving. But my plans changed when I met a boy. We were both so young, and what I thought might last forever ended before it really started. For reasons you'll learn of later, despite the protestations of my aunt, I foolishly rushed into marrying your father who offered me what I thought would be a stable life. But I knew, almost immediately, that with him, I'd live a life of loneliness. When you arrived, I had reason to live again, you brought joy into my life. You always have.

In your final year of school, as I anticipated life without you, I treasured every moment. When you left, home no longer felt like home. I didn't want to be there, alone, without you. Each day, I found myself in your room crying, and knew I couldn't do that for the rest of my life. I missed you and wanted to be closer to you.

My dream of leaving the island has never faded. And now, Tom, finally, I've done it. A month ago, I moved to Glasgow and my life has changed in ways I couldn't have imagined. I'm so happy here, everything is so much better than I ever dreamt it would be. I visit museums and galleries; I have a small circle of friends who I meet regularly. I've even been to dances. I really couldn't be happier.

But, Tom, my son, there is another reason for my happiness. My life has changed in another, more profound way. I expect this will come as a surprise, but, Tom, I am in love. I'm sorry to be revealing this in a letter, but details of how this all unfolded are too complicated to put in writing, so I'll wait and tell you in person.

And, Tom, well, there's no other way of saying it. I am to marry this Saturday and I want you and Lucia to be there. Be assured, he is a good man, kind, interesting, and we laugh together. I love him so much, I'm so immensely proud of him, as I am of you. And he makes me happy, as do you. And so, please do come and share this day with us. Living life in the shadows, as I did on the island, is finally over. Sometimes, when we talk, long, wonderful discussions about art, music, the world, well, he reminds me of you. I'm sure you'll like him.

Tom, do please try and come. I apologise again for such a revelation in a letter and not telling you in person, and for the short notice. But please do try and come.

Love, Mother

Scheduled to leave at 10:30, the Edinburgh to Glasgow train was cancelled. The next train, thirty minutes later, would have us hard pushed to get to the ceremony on time.

"Widows on the island remained widows," I explained to Lucia on the journey to Glasgow.